WARD INVESTIGATION

SEAL's Pretend Girlfriend

SEAL's Pregnant Ex-Wife

SEAL's Fake Relationship

WARD INVESTIGATION : BOOK TWO

SEAL's Pregnant Ex-Wife

USA TODAY BESTSELLING AUTHOR

LESLIE NORTH

BLURB

This Navy SEAL knows danger… but it's nothing compared to fighting to regain true love.

Navy SEAL Lance Ward never thought he'd be in the position of seducing his ex-wife and protecting their unborn child—all while trying to solve his father's murder. Yet, here he is, thanks to Ruth, the only woman who knows how to get under his skin—and under his clothes—in record time. The only problem is, Ruth has *zero* interest in getting back together. But he's not so keen on letting her go a second time.

Ruth gave up on a happily ever after a long time ago. She's not the same naïve young woman she was when she married Lance all those years ago. These days, she's a successful, hard-hitting lawyer… with a soft spot for a certain SEAL who can make her blood sing—and for their unborn child.

But Ruth's in a predicament. She'd hired Lance's father to investigate suspicious deaths and then he'd met the same fate. Now it looks like the bad guys are after her.

As danger nears and her feelings for Lance burn brighter than ever, Ruth realizes it's not just her life at risk… but her heart.

MAILING LIST

Thank you for reading "SEAL's Pregnant Ex-Wife"
(Ward Investigation Book Two)

Get SIX full-length novellas by USA Today best-selling author Leslie North for FREE! Over 548 pages of best-selling romance with a combined 3643 FIVE STAR REVIEWS!

Sign-up to her mailing list and get your FREE books:

www.leslienorthbooks.com/sign-up-for-free-books

CONTENTS

1

Funny how things always circled back around.

Lance Ward got out of his car and stood on the sidewalk in front of a bland-looking office building in downtown Detroit, and took a deep breath. The air smelled crisp and clear with a hint of water from the nearby river. Sun was shining today, though the shadows from the buildings blocked out most of it here. Two months ago, he'd wondered if he'd ever come home again.

Now he was back, with a mission. A personal mission he needed to handle in the next three weeks.

He looked both ways, then jogged across the busy street to the entrance. The place was a little worn and dated, but still functional—and it seemed to be fully occupied. The lobby was full of suits rushing this way and that.

God, he hated these kinds of spaces.

Give him open air and blue skies any day over stuffy boring offices.

It was one of the things he missed most about being boots on the ground with his SEAL team.

Which made the fact he was now stuck working in one of those stuffy boring offices himself these days that much more ironic. And awful. The fact that the office building happened to be the Pentagon didn't make it any more appealing. But he had three more weeks of personal leave away from it, during which he had a job to do, a mystery to solve. It involved his late father, his family, and the woman he was here to see today—his ex-wife, Ruth Becker.

After his father, Gary, had died unexpectedly, Lance and his brothers had struggled to come to terms with the loss—right up until Gary's assistant-turned-partner at his PI business had come forward with her theory: that Gary was murdered. Eventually, they had caught the killer…but then learned that Gary's murder was tied to a larger organization. One that might have set its sights on Ruth, who had hired Gary for the investigation that eventually led to his death. And that was why Lance was here now: because he feared she might be in ongoing danger.

An elevator dinged and he hurried over to get onboard with the others. He pressed the button for the fifth floor and then stood in the corner, a good head taller than anyone else in the car with him. Everyone stared straight forward as they jolted upward.

Soon, he exited the elevator again onto beige carpets that led to a door reading *Becker Law LLC*.

Passing through the door, he found himself faced with a reception desk. He approached, putting on his best charming smile. "Hello, I'd like to see Ruth Becker, please."

The woman behind the desk glanced up from her computer and did a double-take. Lance didn't think much about how he looked, but women seemed to like it and it came in handy at times like this. He'd inherited his height from his dad, as had his two brothers, and they all shared his dark brown curly hair, too. Then the navy had had twenty years to tone and shape him into someone capable of completing any task—even charming his way into a meeting with his ex. He batted his green eyes at the woman openly ogling him now, not above a little flirting if it got him what he needed.

"Is she available?" he asked when the woman didn't respond, leaning an elbow on the desk and widening his smile a bit more, lowering his voice to sound a bit naughtier.

The woman frowned and clicked more keys on her computer. "Name, please?"

"Lance Ward." He straightened a bit. "I don't have an appointment."

"Oh. Um." Pink flushed the woman's cheeks and her frown deepened. "Then I'm sorry, but I'm afraid Ms. Becker is—"

"We're old friends," he said, which was true, if misleading. She'd been his best friend when he'd married her at age eighteen. The friendship had mostly fizzled out after she asked for a divorce when they were twenty-two—he'd been too busy feeling shocked and hurt and discarded to feel all that friendly—but even in the aftermath, their relationship had never been bitter or harsh. They'd just…continued their lives in separate directions, right up until his father's funeral, when he saw her for the first time in years. He gave the woman a look, one that crinkled the corners of his eyes, then winked. "She'll see me."

"One moment, please." The woman swiveled her chair away and picked up the phone receiver to call Ruth. Her tone was too quiet for him to hear much of what was said, but pretty soon the woman hung up and gave Lance a curt nod. "Please have a seat. She'll be with you shortly."

"Thanks." He'd barely made it two steps before a familiar voice echoed from behind him.

"What are you doing here?" Ruth said.

He turned to find her standing outside a doorway down the hall to his right, looking as lovely as ever. He walked over to her, ignoring the receptionist's curious stare following him, and stopped outside her office door where Ruth stood with her arms crossed over the top of her gray blazer. "Uh, hi. Sorry to stop by like this, but we need to talk."

Her dark eyes looked wary. She waited until he got closer to her to whisper, "Is this about our hook-up?"

Damn. Lance had been doing his best to forget that for the past couple of weeks.

God. What the fuck had he been thinking? Well, he hadn't. That was the problem. It had been the day after his dad's funeral. Lance had been wrecked, physically and emotionally. He and his dad had had their share of issues. No lie. But they'd slowly been reconnecting these past few years, talking once a week on the phone about sports and work and other assorted stuff that didn't mean anything really, and everything too, all at the same time. So when he'd gotten the call that Gary was dead, completely out of the blue, it had hit Lance hard. Harder than he'd ever expected.

Then, seeing Ruth again at the funeral, had been... wow. She'd seemed like a ray of light in an otherwise gray, dreary world, and he'd been drawn to her once more like a moth to the proverbial flame. When she'd invited him for a drink the day after the funeral, he'd been compelled to accept. And later, when they'd gone back to her place, falling into bed with her and losing himself in her body felt like a balm to his wounded soul. The way she'd felt under him, around him. The way she smelled, tasted, sounded. So familiar, yet so very new and exciting too after the time apart. It had been like coming home and discovering it all over again.

Focus, dude. Focus.

Lance shook off the memories of their night together and cleared his throat. "It's not about that."

"Too bad," she said with a ghost of a smile. "I had a good time. But you're right. Best to forget about it. But if not that, why are you here? Come to think of it, why are you still in Detroit at all? I thought you went back to DC already."

"I did. My boss needed me to come back for two weeks to handle some things that couldn't wait, in exchange for more time off now. I'm back because there's more going on connected to my father's death—and I won't be leaving until I get to the bottom of it. That's why I'm here. To talk about your meeting with Neal and Lori a few weeks ago."

The color drained from Ruth's pretty face and she blinked up at him a second, then stepped back to wave him inside her office. He didn't miss the way her gaze darted in both directions before she followed him inside and shut the door. Yep. Something was definitely up here. Ruth had a secret, and he was going to find out what.

"I don't know what you want me to say, Lance," she said, not looking at him now as she took a seat back behind her desk. "It was a short meeting, Neal and Lori following up on why I decided to drop my investigation. Why would we need to talk about that?"

"Because I want to know why you lied to my brother and Lori," Lance said gently. Neal had told him that Ruth had seemed spooked during their interview, which had happened just a few days after the funeral. She looked shaken now, too. She'd told Neal at the time that she hadn't gotten any threats connected to the case she'd given Gary…but Neal hadn't believed her, and Lance didn't, either. She was in danger, and she knew it. So why was she lying about it? Didn't she know he'd do anything to help her, protect her?

"I didn't lie. I told them exactly what I'm going to repeat to you now. I hired Gary to double check some facts for me because I suspected my clients were being dishonest with me. I do that a lot. It's routine in my field."

He sighed and stretched out his long legs, making himself comfortable, not intending to budge any time soon as he dropped another bombshell. "Ruth, I'm sure you've seen the papers—you know my dad was murdered and that my brothers and I caught the killer. But what the police kept out of the papers was that the killer was just the trigger man. My dad was poisoned on orders from someone in the mob—poisoned in such a way as to make it look like a heart attack. And we believe it happened while he was investigating the deaths of other people who might also have been poisoned in the same way." She froze and he knew he'd hit a bullseye. He leaned in, holding eye contact with her for this next part, the part he really wanted her to pay attention to. "When Neal and Lori left your office after talking to you, they were tailed. It was *not* by Gary's killer. We have reason to believe it was someone connected to the mob. That was the one and only time they were followed by someone other than the killer, which makes it seem pretty obvious to us that the mob wasn't keeping an eye on them—it was keeping an eye on *you*. And it might still be."

He paused for a minute, letting her absorb all of that. Then he spoke again. "I suspect there's a lot more to this story than what you're telling me. And I think you need to tell me exactly what happened that led to you hiring my dad, and what made you call Lori off and cancel the investigation after he was killed. This isn't going away, Ruth. And if you ignore that—if you refuse to tell me what happened, refuse to let me help—it might just get you killed."

"Lance, I'm—"

"I don't want to see anything happen to you. That's why I'm here. Jesus, Ruth." Lance stood, needing to burn off some of the energy pinballing inside him. "You were always so strong. Strong and brave and determined to do the right thing. Those were some of the things I lov—" He stopped himself before he said the words. It had been too long and there'd been too much water under the bridge to go back there again. Not now. Maybe not ever. He raked a hand through his hair and stared at the books on her shelves until his pulse slowed. Dammit. He needed to get this right. For his dad. For his family. For himself. And for her.

Think, dude. Think.

He exhaled slowly and blinked down at the floor. Something must have happened, something he didn't know about. Some threat or warning or carefully staged "accident" that had made her back down from the investigation she'd started. Must have, because what else would make his brilliant, beautiful, ballsy ex sit down and shut up? The Ruth he'd been married to would never have given in like that without a very good reason. But could he get her to admit it?

Lance wheeled around and stared straight at her. She'd always had a good poker face, but he'd usually been able to crack through it. "Ruth, look me in the eye and tell me the truth. Is someone threatening you?"

The way she blanched said it all.

Shit.

"I can't help you if you won't be honest with me about what's going on." He walked back over to her now, leaning over her desk so only about six inches separated them. "Tell me, Ruth. Tell me what Gary was really looking into for you."

For a moment, Lance thought she might try to evade the question, but then she collapsed into her seat and shook her head. "I hired your dad to look at a series of three clients who'd died of 'heart attacks' after pleading guilty to crimes I was sure they hadn't committed. Crimes that would earn them long sentences, against my advice. They were fairly young and healthy, no underlying health problems, yet they'd all had heart attacks. Seemed hinky as hell to me. So I hired Gary to look into it for me. Then your dad died too. The papers said it was from natural causes and I wanted to believe that was the truth…but they said that about my clients, too. And then, shortly after your dad's passing, I received a warning from a prison contact of mine to drop the whole thing or else something bad would happen to me too, and all the people I care about."

Lance took that in, a confusing mix of emotions washing through him. It was a relief to have Ruth finally open up to him and trust him with the truth. But the truth was just as dark and sinister as he'd feared. The danger was very real, and he had a hell of a lot of work to do in the next three weeks if he was going to wrap this up before he was due back in DC.

"Okay." He sat back and took a deep breath. She'd let him in on her story. He needed to do the same for her. She deserved to have as full a picture of the situation as he could give her. "So, when we caught the guy who'd poisoned Gary, he told us how he did it. He said he was passed a vial of poison that needed to be injected, not ingested. But he couldn't just walk up and inject it into my dad, so he drugged him first. Put a sedative in his coffee to knock him out, then injected him once he was unconscious. In the autopsy, they found the sedative but thought he might have just taken a sleeping pill or something. They didn't notice the injected drug at all."

"Christ." Ruth's eyes looked huge in her pale face. "That's horrible. But it makes a lot of sense."

"Yeah. I suspect your dead clients were probably taken out the same way. Even if they were somehow willing to commit suicide, it's not like they'd be given access to syringes and stuff in prison. It would take another person to inject them and then dispose of the used syringe afterward. I intend to find the person, whoever gave the order to kill my dad in the first place, and take them down." Lance sat forward again. "And to keep you safe. So, until this is over, we'll be working together, okay?"

She opened her mouth, closed it, then opened it again. Finally, she nodded.

"Right." Lance stood and headed for the door. "I'll be in touch."

2

———————

"So, where should we go for dinner?" Ruth asked her friend Collette on the phone the next afternoon. "I hear there's a great new Italian place over on Oakwood we could try."

"Eh. I don't know. I was thinking maybe Asian this time," Collette said. "There's a new sushi bar-slash-Pacific rim fusion opening in Troy near the Somerset Mall. Oh, but speaking of Troy, did I tell you about my firm's newest client?"

Collette Simcoe-Smith was Ruth's best friend from college, and a fellow lawyer. Collette worked in corporate law, while Ruth was in defense. She had also been trying to get Ruth to jump ship and come to work at her firm across town. Collette kept citing the fact that Ruth was seriously undercompensated for the amount of work she put in, which Ruth had to admit was true. Collette also said that corporate law was so much more relaxed, and that Ruth should give it a try sometime. Nice cushy offices, big bonuses, and extravagant lunches, all on their clients' dimes. But Ruth loved her work as a defense attorney and what it lacked in prestige, it more than made up for in worthwhileness. At least for her. She'd much rather know that she'd made a real difference in someone's life, rather than just collect a paycheck until retirement. Not that she looked down on those in her profession who did. That just wasn't her.

Collette went on, telling Ruth about all the impressive clients she'd be able to work with if she came to work with her, and Ruth let her, scrolling through email on her computer as she half-listened to her friend extoll the virtues of her firm. Collette did tend to be a little on the opinionated side, as Ruth's mom always said, and could maybe be a little pushy, but that had never kept them from being friends. In fact, Ruth kind of liked having a person so different from her as a sounding board. Anyway, the monologues about how she should change what she was doing with her life were all in good fun. Collette knew Ruth would never switch the type of law she practiced and besides, Ruth was perfectly content with her practice and a woman didn't just give that up, right?

When her friend switched topics back to food and which restaurant they should choose, Ruth moved from virtual mail to the real thing, sorting through the stack of envelopes her assistant had left on her desk earlier. Most of it was bills, which needed to be forwarded to the accounting department, or invitations to various functions and fundraisers around the city, which she'd have her assistant accept or decline on her behalf depending on who was throwing the shindig. But one envelope in particular caught her eye. The Ward Investigations logo gleamed in silver foil from the corner. Pulse kicking up a notch, Ruth quickly opened it to find a note from Lori Hart, Gary's former assistant who had taken over the practice after his death— along with Neal, the middle Ward brother, who Ruth had heard also happened to be dating Lori. *Found these while cleaning out Gary's stuff,* the note said. *Thought you might like them.*

From inside the envelope, several pictures tumbled out.

Ruth's breath hitched as an image from her and Lance's wedding caught her attention. God. They'd been so young then. Only eighteen. And they'd looked completely in love with each other, dopey heart-eye expressions on their faces. The sad thing was that it was all true, back then. They *had* been completely in love, convinced that they'd spend the rest of their lives together. She sighed, feeling sad. How things changed. Ruth picked up another photo, this one of her and Neal, laughing at the youngest Ward brother, Ryan, because the seven-year-old had been caught sneaking frosting off the back of their wedding cake. And another, with Gary giving her a great big hug. He'd told her then that Lance had been damned lucky to find her. Her chest squeezed tight. Gary had been such a good man. The way he'd died had been wrong. So wrong.

Oh God. If only I'd hired someone else to investigate those cases—or just left the whole thing alone in the first place—Gary would still be alive.

It's my fault he's dead.

Eyes stinging, she shoved the photos and the note back into the envelope, then slid the whole thing into a drawer of her desk. Out of sight, out of mind—or at least, that was the theory. The truth was, she couldn't stop thinking about Gary…and about her inadvertent role in his death. She'd already been feeling guilty after her meeting with Lance yesterday, mainly about not doing more to help them find the mobster who'd ordered the hit. Gary had been great to her, both as a father-in-law and as a PI. She owed him more than she could ever repay, and it felt like she was letting him down now by letting the person behind his death walk free. She tried to tell herself that it wasn't her responsibility, that his sons were taking care of it—and considering that all three were highly trained Navy SEALs, helped along by Lori who was a licensed PI, she was sure that they had it all under control. For her part, she still had the rest of her day to get through, clients to see, cases to prep for. The world didn't stop because of her poor choices.

Unfortunately.

Shit. Just shit.

She grabbed a tissue from the box on her desk and dabbed her eyes, then discreetly blew her nose.

"So, what do you think?" Collette asked, oblivious to Ruth's little meltdown, thankfully.

"Uh…" Crap. Ruth had no idea what her friend had said, and right then she didn't care. "Fine. Sounds good. Listen, I need to go, okay? See you on Thursday. Just text me the address."

She ended the call before Collette could say anything else. Ruth knew she'd hear about it later, but she just didn't have the headspace to talk about dinner plans right now. What she needed was to get her shit together, get off her butt, and go talk to Lance again. Because while she was scared of the threats, she thought less of herself for letting them force her to back down. Gary deserved better than that. And anyway, whatever danger was waiting for her down this path, she wouldn't have to face it alone. With Lance there to protect her, they could bring this bastard down, whoever it was. She and Lance might not be together anymore, but she still trusted him to keep her safe.

And yes. She owed this to Gary. To find the person who ordered his murder and take them down.

She needed to get this guilt off her shoulders so she could get back to the life she'd built for herself.

So she'd help Lance, however he needed, whatever he needed.

Sort of a parting gift for the few good years they'd had together before it all went south.

First, though, she had to rearrange her busy afternoon. A quick phone call to her trusty assistant took care of that, and then she left a little early to head over to Gary's old place. She wasn't sure where Lance was staying, but figured that was a good place to start. As she drove to the house, her mind kept wandering back to those pictures Lori had sent and the wedding from twenty years ago.

Her four years of marriage had started out happy. Yes, they had had to live separately, Ruth heading off to college while Lance had started his career in the navy, but they'd treasured the brief snatches of time they were able to have together. She'd thought, maybe a little naively, that love would get them through anything. But then she'd graduated college and Lance's four-year term had ended…and she'd been forced to take a hard look at their lives that had started her wondering whether they were on the same path at all. Lance had found his calling in the navy, but she'd found her calling in the legal system and had been accepted to Stanford Law School. And she just couldn't see how those two dreams could be compatible.

Staying together would have meant one of them giving up their dream. Namely her. Because there was no way she could be the kind of lawyer she wanted to be while traipsing around the world after her husband's career, always moving from military base to military base with no roots, no stability. Probably couldn't be a lawyer at all, unless she wanted to spend her entire life taking the bar exam over and over, getting certified to practice law everywhere they went. And the kind of law she wanted to practice—where she'd dig in, be part of a community, make a difference—wouldn't be possible. You couldn't have it all, and so she'd had to make a choice.

Ruth turned onto the residential street where Gary's house sat, and sighed. It had been hard. So hard to tell Lance that their marriage had to end. Because he was a good man. One of the best she'd ever known. Smart, fearless, loyal as hell. It was why she trusted him so much. But it was also why they'd gotten divorced. The lives they wanted just didn't align.

By the time she pulled up in front of the house and cut the engine, she was having second thoughts about her unplanned visit. Maybe she should have called first. Or taken more time to think this through. She stared out the window at the porch where she and Lance had had their first kiss back in high school. At the backyard, where they'd cooked out and drunk beer under the stars with their friends. It was where they'd had their first date, too. The big old oak tree was still out front. She remembered when it had been a seedling, Gary out there planting it with the boys, so proud of himself and them.

God. There were so many fond memories here. Things she hadn't thought about for years. Sometimes they felt like another lifetime ago. In some ways, maybe they were a lifetime ago. Things had changed so much since then.

They had changed so much.

Without thinking, she rubbed the sore spot on her chest, right over her heart. Maybe she should just go, leave the Ward family in her past.

No. This was the right thing to do.

She got out and walked up to the door before she could second-guess herself again, rang the bell, and waited. Eventually the door opened and there stood Lance, looking far more gorgeous than any man had a right to. He was dressed in jeans and a T-shirt, his feet bare, hair slightly ruffled like he'd been taking a nap or something. It felt far more intimate than it should have, seeing him like this.

"What are you doing here?" he asked, frowning. His smile was dazzling, but even his frown looked better than it had any right to. Even after all these years, Lance Ward was still the best-looking man she'd ever seen in real life. And that was saying something. Tall, dark, with that whole alpha-protector vibe going on. A lot of gals in town thought Ryan, the youngest Ward brother, was the prettiest one, and maybe they were right—but pretty wasn't what she was after, anyway. She'd take a bit rough and mysterious over movie star gorgeous any day of the week.

"Uh, I was hoping we could talk again. About your dad's case," she added quickly, clearing her throat when those words came out a bit rougher than she'd intended.

Lance hesitated a moment, then sighed and stepped aside to let her in. She stepped past him, catching a hint of soap and fabric softener, mixed with that cologne he'd always liked. Spice and cedar and something a little bit sweet, too. "You know, the more I thought about that, the more I think maybe it's a mistake, bringing you into this."

"No. I don't think it is. I want to do this, Lance. Please." She hesitated a moment, then added, "I need to do this. For Gary." Fighting hard battles was what she did for a living. If anyone could change his mind here, it was her. "And listen, you'll have a better chance of getting this guy with my help. You haven't lived in Detroit in decades, Lance. Things have changed. I've got the connections on both sides of the law, from people I've defended over the years to the attorneys I work with." When he still didn't look convinced, she continued to press her case. "And don't forget that I'm the one who originally spotted the suspicious heart attack pattern in the first place." She set her bag down in the living room and walked over to where he was still standing by the door. "Look, I'll admit that I was scared at first to do this, knowing that the mob is involved, but with you here to keep me safe, we can use my connections and knowledge of this city to get to the truth about your dad's death. I know Lori is working on it too, but she's also got her hands full trying to keep Ward Investigations running. So, what do you say? Are we a team again?"

He looked at her for a small eternity, those pretty green eyes of his unreadable. Then, finally, he nodded. "Okay. But just for this case. That's it." He walked around her and headed for the kitchen, waving for her to follow him. "Come on in here. I've got everything I've collected about the case so far spread out on the table. Take a look and see if I've missed anything."

3

______

"Here are the files I brought," Ruth said the next day as she took a seat beside Lance on the park bench he'd staked out for them and plopped the folders onto his lap. "They're the three former clients I think were poisoned."

Lance carefully moved his sandwich aside to avoid it being squished, then said, "Hello to you too." He looked over at her and noticed she hadn't brought any food, just a bottle of water, even though they had timed this meeting for her lunch break. "Aren't you eating?"

"No. Not very hungry," she said, shrugging. She looked a bit pale and there were dark circles under her eyes. He'd noticed them last night, too, but hadn't asked, not wanting to ruin their tentative accord by getting too personal. He'd thought maybe there'd been a big case at work or something that was keeping her up at night. Now, though, with the not eating thing, he was starting to get a little concerned. Stress wasn't usually enough to make Ruth lose her appetite. At least, it never had been before. Before he could say anything, though, she continued, pointing at the topmost file. "I've been talking to the cellmate of that one. Tony's the one who died most recently. And it was

18

his cellmate who warned me to drop the case. Seems like a good place to start."

"What?" Lance opened the folder and did a quick scan of the information. Anthony Pelash had been the client—and his cellmate was listed as Pat Brown. About as generic a name as you could get. The fact the guy had warned Ruth she was in danger sent up all kinds of red flags. "Oh. Right. Well, let me meet with him. Bet I can get some information out of him. If he knows enough to warn you, then he probably has a pretty good idea of what went down with Tony. Maybe he saw something and can identify some of the players involved. I'd like to know if this was handled by other prisoners with contraband or if someone in a position of authority was involved—maybe a prison guard. Wouldn't be the first time the mob had someone on the take."

"I'd like to know that, too." Ruth took another gulp of water, her fingers trembling slightly. Lance's worry grew. Something was definitely wrong here. None of this was how Ruth usually behaved. Sure, the threats probably had her rattled, but none of the symptoms seemed to match up with how he'd have expected her to react. There was something more at play here. She just kept going on about the case, though. "I don't think Pat will be willing to talk to you, though. He's already faced down Detroit's finest and me, and hasn't spilled a word. As far as I know, the closest he ever came to snitching was what he told me about the danger." She cocked her head and stared out at the playground in front of them. "Although the last time I was there he did seem really scared. Maybe he'll say more now." She shrugged and stared down at her water bottle again. "Maybe it's better if we give him a little bit of room for now, start with the other two first and then come back around to him. Maybe run a background check on them to see if they have any known mob contacts— and also check to see if there are any areas of overlap for all three. Maybe these guys had some connection to the guy who poisoned Gary, too."

"Maybe. I don't know." Lance tossed the rest of his sandwich in the trash bin nearby, his own appetite evaporating under the growing tension in his gut. If something was wrong with Ruth, he wanted answers. He struggled to keep his mind on the case. "Seems like that route might take too long. Do we really have time to do all that research when we could get answers today just from talking to that cellmate? I'm afraid if we don't get more aggressive here, this mobster might cover his tracks and our trail will grow cold. Listen, is everything all right with—"

"I don't think a few extra days will matter." Ruth cut him off, then placed a hand over her stomach, going a bit green. "Uh, let's just take our time and be thorough. Gather more information before going in. That will be better in the long run. We don't want to miss evidence. Besides, it'll take that much time for you to get approved as a visitor at the prison anyway. Then, depending on what we find, you can talk to Pat and ask him more specific questions, based on whatever we uncover. Might be easier to get him to open up if we know exactly what we're looking for. It's not like he's a danger to me, Lance. He's locked up in prison."

He didn't like this one bit—it went against the grain for him to sit back and do research when he wanted to be out there, *doing* something—but he had to admit that she was right. Doing their research would give them more leverage when they finally did start questioning people. And getting that visitor pass would take time. He crossed his arms and nodded. "Fine. What do you think we should do first?"

They stood and started out of the park, and he couldn't help reaching out to steady her a bit by the elbow. She gave him a look and he let his hand drop. Yeah. Okay. Message received. Despite their one-night stand, and their new partnership working on the case, they really weren't on a touchy-feely basis here. It was for the best, even if his hands tingled to take her by the shoulders and demand to know what the fuck was happening with her. They made it almost to the park exit when all of a sudden, Ruth took off running for a trash bin nearby and leaned over to hurl her guts into it. Lance had seen far worse in the SEALs and he stayed by her side, holding her hair for her and rubbing her back, though he doubted she even knew he was there. Being sick to his stomach was his least favorite thing in the world and his heart ached for her being so ill. It also sent his already burgeoning fears skyrocketing. What if she had a serious medical condition? What if the mafia had somehow gotten to her? Slipped her something that was making her sick? Even if this wasn't a deliberate attack, there were still so many things that could be wrong. Before he could stop them, memories swamped his mind of his mother's quick decline from stage four breast cancer found far too late. The old terror and hurt nearly choked him before he tamped it down.

Stop it. It's just puking. That's all.

When she finally straightened, his heart sank. She looked like death warmed over.

"Jesus, Ruth. Are you all right?" He handed her some napkins he'd stuck in his pocket earlier. She looked flushed and flustered, her cheeks bright pink and her eyes watering. When her hands shook too badly to take the napkins, he cleaned her up himself, gently wiping her face before leading her away from the trash bin. Gradually her color improved, and she rinsed her mouth out with the rest of her water.

"I'm fine," she protested, rubbing the back of her hand over her clammy forehead and stepping away from him at last. At least this part was familiar. He knew she hated being fussed over. "It's nothing," she said. "Probably just a bug I picked up somewhere. I've been feeling off for the last couple of days. Headache, fatigue, upset stomach. All the normal flu stuff."

Lance wasn't convinced. And he felt the need to be extra cautious, with all the poison shenanigans going around these days. "Has anyone else you have contact with had similar symptoms?"

They started out of the park, Ruth trying to act like everything was fine. "No, not that I can think of, but that doesn't matter. I could've gotten it anywhere. Why?" They stopped at the corner and waited for the light to turn, Ruth giving him an annoyed side glance. "Why are you being so weird about this?"

"Because," he said, doing his best to stay calm and not spook her, even though it was beginning to feel like it totally was a huge deal. His heartbeat kicked higher. "Look. I don't want to freak you out here, Ruth, but we're dealing with people who have other people drugged and killed. I don't want to risk the same thing happening to you. You already said they threatened you, so…"

The light turned green, and they started across the street to her building.

"I think you should go to the hospital and let them run some tests, just to be sure," Lance said, taking her arm as they reached the curb in front of her address. He didn't want her getting back into her office and then collapsing alone where no one would find her until it was too late. "Please. For me." At her "seriously" look, he added, "You're right. It could be nothing at all. The flu. A cold. Whatever. Or," he nudged her closer to the building out of the way of pedestrian traffic and lowered his voice, "it could be exposure to some kind of slow-acting poison."

"Honest to God, Lance—" she started to protest, but he cut her off.

"Listen. I could be completely overreacting here and I really hope I am." He put his hands on her shoulders. "But what if the mob somehow found out you're looking into this case again?"

"How? How would they find out?"

"I don't know. A leak in your office or something. Or maybe they saw you come to my dad's house and got suspicious. How sure are you that you weren't followed? Anyway, what if they found out and came after you, huh?" He searched her gaze. "Are you willing to risk your life on that? Are you?"

Lance prayed she'd go along with him on this, because he really didn't want to force her to go get checked out, but he would if it came down to it. It was one thing risking his own life. He refused to do that with Ruth.

Finally, though, she rolled her eyes and gave a curt nod, and he could breathe a little easier. "Fine. I'll go. But you're paying the bill for my visit. And seriously, I'm sure you're wrong about me being poisoned. I think I'd notice if someone jabbed a syringe into my arm, okay?"

There was no guarantee the mob would stick to using a syringe, especially since her symptoms didn't seem anything like what had happened to his dad. They could have used anything—including a poison they could slip into her food—but he wouldn't bring that up. She'd agreed. That was what mattered. "Okay." He steered her toward his car parked down the block. He was still worried as hell, but hoped a little gentle teasing would help take the edge off. "Why are you so concerned about the bill, though? Don't you have insurance? Big fancy lawyer and all?"

"I'm not that fancy." She waited for him to unlock the door, then climbed inside his nondescript gray rental sedan. "But yes, I have insurance. I still owe copays and deductibles, though, and..." She gave him another look and he was just now realizing how much he'd missed those over the years. "Just shut up and get in the damned car and get me to the emergency room before I throw up all over your nice clean interior."

4

Ruth felt like an idiot, lying there in the examination room in the ER, waiting for the doctor to come back and talk to her after running some tests. Seriously. It was just a bug. Lance was over-reacting, as usual. He might be a Navy SEAL, but the same qualities that made him great at his job also made him tend to blow things out of proportion sometimes. Besides, she highly doubted she'd been poisoned. She definitely would have noticed if someone stuck a needle in her arm and shot her up with something. And even if the mafia had decided to switch to a different poison and try to get her to ingest it, there was surely no way they could have gotten it to her. She'd only eaten stuff she'd made herself the last four days.

No. This was nothing. Well, nothing more sinister than a stomach bug or the flu. Definitely not related to what happened to Gary. Honestly, the more she thought about it, maybe it was early-onset menopause. Her doctor had warned her it might be coming, after all. She wasn't completely sure about the symptoms, but she'd heard that the hormone changes could really put your body through the wringer, so fatigue and nausea didn't seem implausible. Also, she'd missed her last period and she normally was like clockwork, so…

She sighed and stared up at the ceiling, the cacophony of monitors and talking and people rushing back and forth echoing around her. Lance had wanted to come back here with her, but she'd said no. She was already embarrassed to have thrown up in front of him. God. Figured that would happen. At least he hadn't been a dick about it.

In fact, he'd been pretty sweet, holding her hair and rubbing her back and all. And while it didn't make up for the mortification of tossing her cookies in a public park trash can for all to see, including her ex-husband, even Ruth had to admit it had been nice to have someone there who was kind and concerned about her. She gave a little smile, picturing him out in the waiting room, prowling around, restless and worried on her behalf. If she was honest, she'd sort of missed that—having someone in her corner. She'd been on her own for a very long time.

Her memories drifted back to their first date. He'd called to cancel because his youngest brother was sick and Lance hadn't wanted to leave Ryan alone while their dad was out working. So Ruth had surprised him by coming over with a picnic. They'd eaten in the back-yard, with Lance going inside every once in a while to check on Ryan. Good times.

A fond ache pinched her chest, remembering. Lance was a really good guy. Always dedicated to the people he loved. He was different from any other man she'd ever known, before or since. Too bad they just couldn't work things out between them.

"Ms. Becker?" the doctor said before slipping back into her room through the curtains. He had a tablet in his hands, which he was glancing over as he spoke. "Looks like I've got some good news for you. We've gotten your test results back and it's not poison or an infection." He tapped his screen and glanced up at her, smiling. "According to this, you're pregnant."

Ruth blinked at him, not understanding. "I'm sorry. What?"

"Pregnant. Both your urine and blood tests were positive. Based on the levels of HcG in your system, I'd say approximately four to five weeks along…"

The doctor kept talking, but Ruth wasn't listening anymore. Her mind was racing way too fast for that. Pregnant. No. That couldn't be right. It wasn't possible. She was thirty-eight years old for Christ's sake, and she'd had sex *once* in the past six months. Things like this didn't happen to people their age. And yes, fine. Maybe that night with Lance one day after the funeral they hadn't been as careful as they should have been, contraceptive-wise, but come on. It was one time. They'd both been vulnerable and had way too much to drink.

Her temples were throbbing now, and Ruth sat up, swinging her legs over the side of the gurney to stare at the shiny linoleum floor below, still trying to wrap her head around what the doctor had just said. What. The. Hell. Were they going to do? Sure, back in the day, there'd been a time when she really wanted kids. In fact, she and Lance used to daydream about being parents. But then they'd gotten divorced. She'd dated in the years since then, but none of those relationships had ever gotten serious enough for kids to even be a consideration, and she'd gradually just put that dream away. Nowadays, it just wasn't on her radar anymore. She had so many demands on her time. She wasn't sure she could handle one more. Especially one of this magnitude. And co-parenting with Lance? How would that even work?

Oh God. She put her hands over her face.

What the hell am I going to do?

The doctor had finished talking and was now handing her paperwork. "These are your discharge papers, Ms. Becker. I included a prescription for some pre-natal vitamins for you to start and I recommend you get an appointment with an OB/GYN at your earliest convenience, if you aren't already established with someone. At your age, there can be more risks with pregnancy, so they'll want to monitor you more closely."

She took the papers he handed her, fingers numb, and managed to ask, "What about the nausea?"

"There's information in there on that, too—tips on ways to manage it," he said, starting out of the curtains again. "Sorry. Don't mean to rush but we've got some accident victims on the way and we're short-staffed. All hands on deck. Have a good night and congratulations again!"

He left and Ruth just sat there a moment, too stunned to move. Eventually she pulled herself together, and then she was on her way back out to the waiting room where Lance was pacing a hole in the floor.

"What did they say?" he asked, rushing over to her as soon as she came through the automatic doors.

Ruth took a deep breath and forced a smile she didn't feel. "Well, it's not poison."

"Good." He narrowed his gaze on her, always too damned perceptive for his own good. "That's good...right? You don't look happy about it."

She had no idea how she felt—or how she was going to tell him. For now, it was all she could manage to get out the words, "Yes, yes. It's good."

It really wasn't, though. Not in Lance's book, anyway. The whole ride home, she didn't say anything, just stared out the window as Lance drove. He kept glancing over at her periodically, hoping she'd talk, but nope. She just sat there all silent and pensive.

His instincts were going haywire. Something major was going on and he wished she'd just tell him what it was, because his mind kept imagining ever-increasingly fatal scenarios to fill in the blanks. Her health wasn't his business. He knew that. But ever since losing his mom when he was just ten years old, he was paranoid. Couldn't stop imagining worst-case scenarios. It was why his brain had gone immediately to poison back in the park. It was why it kept going to…

No. Stop. He had to get a grip on this because it wasn't helping anyone.

Sometimes people just didn't want to talk about things.

The silence was deafening, though. Even the radio didn't help. So, after awhile, he cleared his throat and tried again. "Hey, Ruth. I know this is none of my business. We're not married anymore. But if it's something more serious going on, I want you to know I'm still here for you. I'll be in Detroit for the next few weeks and whatever you need, I'll do. Even if it's just to talk."

A beat passed. Then two. Finally, she said, "I'm not sick. I'm pregnant. And you're the father."

The words took a second to penetrate his brain.

I'm pregnant and you're the father…

They swirled around, getting more tangled by the second. When he was younger, he'd wanted a kid of his own so bad. He'd always thought he and Ruth would have a whole houseful of them someday, once their careers were established, once they'd settled down together. Then they'd gotten a divorce and it had broken him. Her asking for it had come completely out of the blue for him, and he'd been devastated. The last thing he wanted now was to set himself up for another situation where she could change the rules on him and break his heart all over again. But, if putting some trust in Ruth to stick to whatever co-parenting plan they worked out was the price he had to pay to have a baby of his own, then…

Struggling to keep his voice as neutral as possible, Lance asked, "What do you want to do?"

"I haven't decided yet," she said, her tone flat. She stared down at her hands in her lap, not at him.

"Well, if you decide to keep it, I'm all in on co-parenting." Blood thundered loud in his ears and Lance wondered if he was talking louder because of it. He hoped not. The last thing he wanted to do was scare her even more, because she already looked terrified. If he hadn't been driving, he'd have put his arms around her and hugged her. But as it was, he just squeezed the wheel tighter in his hands.

"Be hard to co-parent with us living in two different cities. Hell, two different states," she said, shaking her head. "God, this is such a horrible time for me to be pregnant. I've got so much going on at work, and we've got the mafia coming after us and poisoning people."

His heart sank as Ruth turned to logic. She always did this whenever she thought a problem was too complicated to solve or too hard to fight through. He cleared the lump of dread from his throat and forced out the words, even though they hurt like hell. "It's your decision, about the pregnancy. But if you want to keep it, we'll find a way to make it work. I swear. We'll do it together. You won't be alone." He inhaled deeply, needing to say it. "Sometimes you just have to be bold and leap, Ruth. There's never a good time for this. There'll always be things to do or stuff in the way."

They reached her house and he parked in the driveway, then cut the engine. The neighborhood was peaceful this time of day, and everything was calm and quiet. Ruth took a deep breath, then another, before raising her head and meeting his gaze. "I want this baby."

Lance couldn't contain his smile as he reached over and took her hand. "Okay then. Me too."

Now all he had to do was figure out how to keep his promise and make this work.

5

———

By the next evening, after playing it cool in front of Ruth for nearly twenty-four hours, Lance was going a little nuts trying to tamp down all his feelings about the news. He needed to tell someone else or it felt like he was going to burst. So he got in the car and drove over to the house his brother Neal shared with Lori.

It was around seven when he got there, and when Neal answered the door Lance immediately felt guilty because it looked like Neal was dressed up for a night out.

"Dude, this really isn't a good time," Neal said, then stopped, frowning. "Are you okay?"

Lance had thought he was keeping it together pretty well, but apparently not. Or maybe Neal was just that good at reading him. "I've got some stuff going on I really need to talk to somebody about and—"

"Who is it?" Lori called from another room.

"It's Lance," Neal called back. "I told him we were on our way out."

Lori stepped into view and gave him a careful once-over. She didn't seem to like what she saw, either. "I don't think we're going anywhere tonight, sweetie. Lance, come on in."

Neal gave a deep sigh and stepped back to wave Lance in. The two of them followed Lori into the living room where they all sat down.

Lance gave her a sheepish look. "Sorry to ruin your plans."

"Plans schmans." She waved off his apology and grinned. "What brings you by?"

He just blurted it out. "Ruth's pregnant. It's mine."

A flurry of congrats and hugs and back slaps occurred, followed by an awkward silence.

Neal frowned. "You don't seem as happy about this as I thought you'd be."

"I am," Lance said, resting his forearms on his knees, his hands dangling between his legs. "Really. I've always wanted a kid. But there's a lot of stuff to think about now and it's got me more than a little freaked out."

Lori scooted closer to him on the sofa, putting her hand on his shoulder. "We're here for you. Whatever you need."

"Thanks." He was grateful for the support. "I'm just thinking about how we'll make this work. It seems like it would be easiest if we were in the same city, but that would mean one of us would have to move. I'm eligible for retirement with full benefits in a few months, and I've been bored stiff since they promoted me to my desk job, so I'm kind of thinking it should be me who rearranges stuff. But then I think about what a great place DC is, with all the historic landmarks and free museums. Not to mention the fact that none of our family members have been murdered there." He waited for the collective chuckle to die down before continuing. "Also, with a baby on the way, now probably is not the best time for me to quit my career, but I can't see Ruth leaving her practice to move to DC with me, so…"

Neal gave him a serious stare. "Okay. You've talked a lot about the logistics of it all, but what about emotionally? How do you feel about becoming a dad?"

Lance took a deep breath, the tightness in his chest that had been there since he'd first gotten the news last night easing a bit. A grin formed on his face, only widening the more certain he was. "Honestly, I'm excited as hell." He laughed, then sobered. "But I'm also scared to trust it."

"Why?" Neal asked, looking confused.

"I just don't know how things will work with Ruth and me." Lance sighed and leaned back against the cushions, scrubbing a hand over his face. "That's the thing that's got me torn up the most. Like I said, I've always wanted this. To have a kid of my own. Ruth and I used to talk about it all the time. I know she'll make a great mom, too. So, to have this opportunity now, with Ruth, after all these years, it's…" He shook his head and closed his eyes. "The thing that gets me, though, is what if she quits on me again?"

"Quits on you?" Lori said. "How?"

She hadn't been around back then when the whole divorce happened, so he needed to fill her in. It still hurt, though, even after all these years, so Lance went with a few bullet points rather than a full rundown. "We got married right out of high school, but had to live separately—I went into the navy, she went to college. Four years later, she got into law school at Stanford. It was time for me to re-enlist in the Navy. I thought we'd be fine continuing to do things long distance. But Ruth wasn't on board with that. She divorced me, saying she needed to go lead her own life."

"Oh gosh. I'm sorry," Lori said.

"It's fine," he said, though it really wasn't. "The thing is, when things got tough between us back then, Ruth just gave up. And what scares the shit out of me now is, what if she does it again? Worse, what if I end up a single parent like Dad was, and I end up screwing up my own kid because of it?"

"Dude." Neal reached a leg over and kicked him lightly on the shin. "That's bullshit and you know it."

"Maybe." Lance shrugged, while Lori excused herself to go to the kitchen and get them all some drinks—and, transparently, to give the brothers a chance to hash this out. Neal leaned forward, scowling now.

"I don't want to hear anything about you not being a good parent, okay?" he said, sounding dead serious. "Dad was screwed up in a lot of ways after losing Mom, but you were the one who was there for me and Ryan. You were our parent—the only one we could count on—and you were fantastic at it. You're going to rock this thing."

Lance couldn't help but smile, moved by his brother's faith in him. Though that brought up another question…

"I'm not sure whether I should get credit or blame for Ryan. You've noticed that he's been acting weird lately, right? It's not just me?"

"Definitely not just you," Neal said. "For starters, he's been home longer than any bereavement leave I've ever heard of, but he refuses to talk about when he's going back."

Lance frowned. "When I tried to ask him about it, he got kind of defensive and left. Said he was going to the movies or some shit."

"I wonder if—" Before Neal could finish, Lori returned with their drinks, and he decided to let it drop. Lori was family now, but it still felt like the kind of concern to be kept between brothers for the moment.

The ringing of Lance's phone cut him off before he could introduce a new topic of conversation. Lance held up a finger and pulled it out of his pocket, surprised to see Ruth's number on the display. She'd mentioned earlier that she was meeting a friend for dinner that night, so he hadn't expected to hear from her again until tomorrow. Something must be wrong. He answered right away, his pulse kicking up a notch. "What's going on? Are you okay?"

Ruth's voice was hard to make out given the noise behind her. It sounded like she was calling from a rowdy bar somewhere. "I'm fine. But I was walking home after dinner and it seemed like someone was following me. I ducked into a pub along the way, it's called Barlow's, but I'm afraid to leave—I'm worried that whoever was after me is still out there."

He could hear the fear in her voice and it galvanized him. He signaled to his brother that he needed to leave ASAP and Neal just nodded and got the door for him. He'd explain things to them later. Right now, Ruth needed him. "Stay where you are. I'm on my way."

Twenty minutes later, he entered the pub and scanned the crowd for Ruth. He finally spotted her in a booth near the corner and rushed over, sliding into the seat across from her. "You okay?"

"Yes." She sipped the glass of sparkling water in front of her and gave him an apologetic look. "I'm sorry for calling you. It's probably nothing, but I could've sworn there was a car following me. I even think I saw it circle the block a couple of times after I came in here. That's why I got a booth away from the windows, out of sight."

"Good thinking." Lance pulled out his phone. "Did you happen to get a license plate number?"

"Yep." She slid a napkin across the table to him. "Well, part of it anyway."

"Okay." He texted Neal with the info and asked if he and Lori would run the number and see what they could find. Then he put his phone away and took Ruth's hand across the table. She might have said she was fine, but she still looked a bit too pale and nervous for his peace of mind. Her skin felt soft and warm against his. "Listen. It might be better, at least until we wrap up this case, for you to drive places instead of walk. Or if you don't like driving, then use public transit—go for stops with lots of people around. Okay?"

She nodded.

"Please don't think I'm trying to tell you what to do or anything," he felt like he needed to say, knowing how independent she was. "It's just that from a security perspective, I think you'll be safer that way. Also, please call me again if you need me. Any time. If you're scared or you think something isn't right, I want to know about it. We're partners in this, remember? You don't have to tough it out alone. I'm here for you."

With that Ruth stood. At first, Lance thought maybe she was going to tell him to shove it where the sun didn't shine and walk out, but instead, she leaned over and hugged him. It was the first time she'd done that since his dad's funeral, and it felt damned good. Also surprised the hell out of him, so it took him a second to hug her back. When he did, though, he held on tight. By the time they pulled back, he was feeling about ten degrees warmer and a whole lot happier.

Ruth slid back into her side of the booth and started talking about the case again. Or rather, if they should drop it completely.

"I mean," she said, "I hate to stop an investigation before it's done, but what if someone really was following me out there? The danger might already be picking up and now," she stopped, placing a hand on her abdomen almost absently, like she didn't realize what she was doing, "I don't want to risk the baby." She looked up at Lance. "And I don't want anything to happen to you either. I don't want our child growing up without a father."

Lance leaned back, considering it.

"All I'm saying is," Ruth continued, "you've got a cushy job in DC. I'm an attorney. We're not cops or PIs. Why don't we just drop this whole thing? Or maybe turn it over to Neal and Lori to handle, since that's what they do?"

He sighed. "Neal and Lori are already involved. But I do think the more people we've got working on this thing the faster it's going to get solved. And if people are following you, Ruth, which I think they are, then that's even more reason to get this solved so they stop." He exhaled slowly and squinted out at the bar, all neon and tacky crap hanging on the walls. Booze and bad decisions filled the air. He didn't want to make another one. "I understand where you're coming from, Ruth. I do. But I can't just drop this. One, I owe it to my dad. And two, I truly believe that catching the guy who ordered the hit and taking him down is the only way to keep us all safe in the long run. You don't have to be a part of it, but I'm going to keep working on it. What else do I have to do during my three weeks here?" He glanced up at the wall behind her. "Well, two and a quarter now."

Ruth chuckled and shook her head. "I guess." Then her demeanor changed to something fierce and determined. "But I swear to God, Lance," she growled, her voice rough and sexy. "If you go and get yourself killed on this case, I will never forgive you. Our child needs you. I need you. Understand?" Man, he loved it when she got all mama bear on him.

Lance bit back a grin and gave her his best military salute. No way was he going anywhere until this was all over. "Yes, ma'am!"

6

———————

The next night, Ruth was over at Gary's house again, working late with Lance to try and cross-reference all the known associates of her poisoned clients. So far, they hadn't found any shared connections.

Stiff and restless, she stretched, then set aside her laptop to lean over and peer at Lance's screen from where he sat beside her on the sofa. "Have any luck yet?"

"No," he said, his gaze narrowed on the information he was scrolling through. "I'm actually taking a break from the lists."

"Really?" She sat back and yawned. "What are you looking at, then?"

"Researching what happens during the first trimester of pregnancy."

He said it so nonchalantly, but her heart melted a bit anyway. Part of her thought it was so sweet of him to do that. A lot of guys she knew would be scared off by the details of pregnancy. She had friends whose husbands got grossed out or weirded out by any discussion of how their bodies were changing or how the babies were developing. Lance wasn't her husband anymore, had the perfect excuse to not get too involved, and yet he was diving into this wholeheartedly. It was really, really attractive and it had her remembering all those fantasies she used to have about the two of them raising a family together. She almost started to wonder if that might be a possibility for them after all.

On the other hand, there was still a big part of her—the logical part—that was far more wary. There was a reason their marriage had fallen apart in the first place, after all. Just because he was looking up info about the baby, that didn't mean anything beyond his interest in their child. It wasn't the same as having interest in *them,* as a couple. And even if he was still interested in her, wanted a closer relationship for the two of them, how would that work? She still didn't think he was the kind of person who was willing to walk away from his military career—and she certainly had no plans to leave Detroit. It would take a lot of negotiation and compromise to figure out a workable path forward. And would he be willing to put in that effort for her? Would he ever fully trust her again after she walked away all those years ago?

Not that she'd really blame him if he didn't. She didn't have the best track record with trust, herself—mainly because it had always been a struggle for her to believe that she was allowed to dream big, to reach for the stars, to trust that things would work themselves out. In her experience, life rarely worked out that way.

If she closed her eyes, she could still recall the fight she'd overheard between her mom and her grandmother when she was ten. Her mom had wanted to go to college then—even though she was in her twenties, with a kid—but Grandma had told her that was ridiculous. That you couldn't go back to when you were eighteen and change things. Her mom had made her decisions—and they included her misguided choice as a high school senior to go to a college party, get drunk, and hook up with a boy she couldn't quite remember the next day. After that, she had to live with the consequences of that decision—which meant being a mother to Ruth and scaling back her other dreams to match her circumstances. Mom had never been especially great at that, which was why Ruth had been mostly raised by her grandparents, but she'd stopped talking about college and had managed to look only a little bitter and resentful when Ruth had headed off first to undergrad and then to graduate school.

She'd always felt guilty about that. One more thing to add to the list.

It was only in the last few years that she and her mom had gotten to a good place. Her mom was driving an Uber now and had built herself a surprisingly successful career as a voiceover actress. They saw each other on holidays, and as long as no one brought up anything controversial, like college or marriage, it was all good. Her mom had even met someone, a dentist named Greg. They were longtime partners and he seemed to have a mellowing effect on her mom, which was great. Everything had turned out about as well as it could—but it had taken everyone managing their expectations first. If you dreamed too big, you set yourself up to be disappointed.

Ruth sighed and rested her head back against the cushions. She'd like to get to a good place with Lance too—especially now, with the baby on the way—but she'd have to make sure to keep her expectations in check. They weren't impulsive eighteen-year-olds anymore, rushing into marriage. They were practical, grounded adults, and they knew enough to face facts and be realistic.

And like Grandma always said, you couldn't go back and rewrite the past.

All you could do was move forward.

And their forward meant getting this case solved, not getting all misty-eyed over a bunch of memories. Ruth straightened and picked up her lukewarm tea. "We should concentrate on the case now. It's why I'm here. You can google baby stuff later."

Lance looked over at her from atop his screen, the greenish glow highlighting all the planes of his handsome face. Not that she noticed. Nope. "I hit a dead end with the connection angle. Nowhere else to go there. What I really want to do is talk to Pat Brown and see if we can figure out who injected your client with poison. Or at least who convinced Tony to plead guilty to the crime in the first place."

"Well." She stood to reheat her tea in the microwave for the eleventy-billionth time. "I think you're right." She ignored his told-you-so look. "What? It happens, rarely. Anyway. Your visitor pass should be ready tomorrow. I pulled some strings, so we can go to the prison tomorrow afternoon and talk to Pat."

Visiting hours at FCI Milan were about as cheerful as you'd expect for a federal correctional institution. After going through the security gates and metal detectors, both she and Lance stood with their arms out for pat-downs, then were led into a large room with metal picnic tables bolted to the floor. There were no pictures or other decorations on the starkly whitewashed cinder block walls, just a few high windows letting in the afternoon light. The guard parked them at a table near the corner with instructions to sit tight while he fetched Pat Brown for them. Ruth had been here countless times before, to speak with clients or contacts, but from the look on Lance's face, it was a first for him.

There were several other tables occupied as well. Families with small kids sat on one side, while the husband/father prisoner they were there to visit—dressed in a bright orange jumpsuit and handcuffs—sat on the other. FCI Milan was a minimum-security prison, filled with mainly low-level offenders, which was another thing that made the deaths of her contacts stand out. In a maximum-security place, filled with murderers, an inmate death here and there wasn't as uncommon.

But Milan held mostly drug-related offenders, some petty criminals and white-collar perps who were serving time for things like embezzling. Nothing too heinous.

Lance was staring at a couple across the room from them. A woman was holding a toddler, clearly encouraging the little guy to interact with his father. But the boy was staring at the man across from him like he had no idea who he was. Given the guy might have been locked up for years, it was entirely possible the kid didn't recognize his father at all. "God. How can people live like that?"

"It's hard," Ruth agreed, her heart pinching for the family. Keeping low-level offenders out of prison and getting them into rehab programs where they could get the help they needed was one of the reasons why she did what she did. She had no idea what crime the man opposite them had committed to end up in there, but chances were good his life would be better improved by rehab or job training or something other than sitting in a cell for fifteen hours a day. She started to say more, but the sound of a metal door creaking open nearby stopped her.

The guard led Pat Brown in and sat him down on the bench across from them before securing the chain attached to his handcuffs to a ring bolt at the center of the table. Pat looked about the same as the last time Ruth had seen him. Thirty, a bit heavy-set but muscled. White, with curly brown hair and freckles on his face. Not exactly the kind of guy you'd think of when picturing a criminal. He'd always reminded her a bit of Danny DeVito. Of course, when you committed theft for a living, it probably helped to have a face that kind of blended into the crowd.

Pat hiked his chin at Ruth, then glanced at Lance. "Who's he?"

"This is Lance Ward, Pat. He's helping me out on a case." She smiled, glad to see Pat was acting a bit less nervous than the last time they'd talked. "We were wondering if we could ask you some more questions about what happened when Tony died."

And just like that, the nerves were back. Pat visibly paled and his gaze darted around the room before returning to Ruth. "No," he said, his voice barely above a whisper. "I don't wanna talk about that anymore."

Lance took a deep breath, then looked over at the guy and his family in the corner. "How do you do this, man? Be in here all day and not go nuts?"

A beat passed, then two, before Pat sat back and his tense shoulders slumped a bit. "Eh, you get used to it. Work, eat, rec room, back to sleep."

"Is that what happened the day Tony died?" Ruth put in, not willing to give up so easily. "Was it just a normal day? Or did something else happen? Something out of the ordinary?"

The question seemed to catch Pat off guard. He hesitated, then said warily, "Yeah. It was a normal day. At least, it was for me—Tony had to go into court for some paperwork thing with his guilty plea. But you know that; you were there with him. I was out in the yard when he got back. By the time I got back to our cell, he was dead. That's all there is to it. When are you going to drop this already? He had a heart attack—it happens."

Ruth decided to take a chance on trusting him with a little more. "We don't think it really was a heart attack, Pat. We think he might have been drugged, injected with something that would mimic a heart attack."

"Drugged?" Pat's eyes went wide, but Ruth couldn't tell if he was surprised to hear about the drugs or surprised to hear that she *knew* about the drugs. "I don't got anything to say about that," he added hastily. "Looked like a heart attack to me, and that's what the doc said, too."

"He wasn't the only one," Lance added. "We believe there were others who died the same way. Have you heard anything about that?"

"No," Pat said, but he sounded worried. "Do you have any suspects?" When neither she nor Lance answered, his eyes got wider. "Oh, God. Am I in danger too?"

Ruth leaned forward, hoping to get this back on track. "Pat, I need you to concentrate here, okay? I'll do everything I can to keep you safe, but you have to talk to me. Did Tony ever tell you why he pled guilty against my advice?"

"I don't know." He scowled down at his hands atop the table. "I don't know anything about that and I don't know anything about the money."

Money? This was the first Ruth had heard about that. She looked up and locked eyes with Lance, then returned her attention to Pat. But from the look on his face, he already knew he'd said too much.

Still, she had to try. "What money, Pat?"

"No." He shook his head, sending his too-long, ruffled hair flying around his head. "I got nothing else to say."

"Okay." Ruth signaled the guard and he came over to unhook Pat. "But if you think of anything else, please let me know. It's important."

The guard led the man away and she and Lance got up to leave. They hadn't learned much, but she still had a surge of triumph inside. From the sparkle in Lance's eyes, she knew he felt it too. They'd just gotten their first real clue.

7

The next morning, Lance was up early, making breakfast for him and Ryan. As he cooked, he also tried to figure out a way they could get a look at Ruth's dead client Tony's finances. There was a very good chance the money itself might be gone now, but if they could find a paper trail that proved he'd been paid by the mob, then…

He sighed and flipped the pancakes in the pan. Or maybe it was better to approach this from the other end of things. Try to figure out who would have benefitted from Tony going to jail, then attempt to look at what their mob connections were. Who was truly guilty of the crime Tony was charged with?

"Hey," Ryan said, slouching into the kitchen looking moody as hell and making a beeline for the coffeemaker. "What are you making?"

"Pancakes and bacon," Lance said, putting the finished flapjack on a plate and pouring more batter into the pan. "Have a seat. They'll be done in a second."

"Eh." Ryan shook his head. "Not really hungry. Besides, I don't have time for breakfast today."

Lance stilled, setting the batter aside. After his conversation with Neal the other night about their youngest brother's suspiciously long bereavement leave, he'd decided it was time to get some answers. There was something going on, his SEAL instincts were going haywire about it, and Lance intended to find out what the hell it was.

"Yeah?" he said, shutting off the stove and turning to face his brother. "You're busy? With what? Getting ready to return to your SEAL team? Because don't think for a second that Neal and I haven't noticed you've been here for fucking ever."

Ryan's posture stiffened beneath the ratty old T-shirt he wore to bed. He'd had that thing since high school. Maybe those pajama bottoms too, seeing as how the plaid flannel was faded to a dingy gray and the bottom hem was fraying. Still, they looked comfy and it wasn't like they were putting on a fashion show or anything here. Ryan cleared his throat and stared down into his coffee cup. "I told you. It's fine. I'm here until we've got this whole situation squared away."

"Uh huh." At first, Lance hadn't really questioned it, but no one got leave for this long, no matter what kind of situation they were dealing with at home. Ryan was definitely hiding something. Lance's heart sank. He pushed away from the counter and walked over to take a seat across from Ryan, forcing his inner concern down a notch and willing his voice to stay calm. He took a deep breath, then said, "Look, it's been over a month since Dad's funeral. And I really want to believe you, Ryan, but honestly. No one gets leave that long, not even for a death in the immediate family, no matter the size of the estate there is to settle." He waited a beat or two. "Tell me what's going on with you. Maybe I can help."

Ryan smiled. It looked sincere, but Ryan was an excellent liar, the one their father had trained from a young age to help him blend in when Gary was discreetly scouting for information. He knew exactly what to say and do to shift a conversation in whatever direction he wanted it to go. It took a hell of a lot of stubbornness to get him to admit anything he didn't want to admit.

"What," Ryan said, his tone warm and teasing, "you think I went AWOL or something? Come on, you know I'd never do that. I promise, my CO knows exactly where I am. It's cool, bro. Seriously. Now can we stop fussing over me and focus on the case? Lori called. Said the car Ruth thought might've been following her matched the description of one that was recently stolen. Whoever took it ditched it, though. It was found yesterday, so don't bother keeping an eye out for it. She said the police haven't arrested anyone yet, so no word on whether the thief has any ties to the mob."

Lance nodded, and considered letting the subject of Ryan's situation drop the way his brother so clearly wanted him to. But no, Neal had been right. He'd helped raise these guys. He was never going to stop looking out for them, whether they wanted him to or not. There wasn't a trick in their books he didn't know. "You know you can tell me anything, right?" he said, giving it one more try. "I'm here for you, no matter what."

His brother blinked at him, green eyes like his own. "Yeah, of course I know that. And when I've got something to say, you'll be the first to know. But back to what's important—how's the rest of your case going?"

Lance thought about arguing that Ryan was important to him, but he sensed that it wouldn't do any good. Better to just give in for now. If he kept pushing, Ryan would just withdraw. The little brat was damn slippery when he wanted to be. Living under the same roof with him was no guarantee that he'd ever lay eyes on his brother if Ryan didn't want to be seen. So he got up and returned to the stove, finishing the last few pancakes and bacon.

"The case is…" Lance took a deep breath. "…going. I'm trying to come up with a new angle. What I want to do is shift our investigation towards why the mob would have wanted Ruth's client Tony dead and who might have bribed him to plead guilty. Except I have no idea how to find out who else was a suspect in his case—who might have really committed the crime."

"Hmm." Ryan gulped more coffee, then squinted out the window across from him, the light streaming in from the rising sun growing brighter by the second. "One of my old high school ROTC buddies, Isaac Trapnell, is a cop with Detroit PD. I could call him. See if he'd be willing to give you a peek at the files."

"That might work," Lance said, dishing up the last pancake and putting the pan in the sink before setting a plate in front of his brother, ignoring his earlier refusal. Who didn't love pancakes and bacon? Ryan couldn't get enough of that shit growing up. He got his own plate and a cup of coffee, then took his seat across from his brother again. Lance hid his grin at the fact that half Ryan's stack and two of the four slices of bacon were already devoured off his brother's plate before Lance had even taken his first bite. *Not hungry, my ass.* He dug into his own food, pausing between bites to say, "Yeah. If you could contact your friend and ask him, that would help. Thanks. Appreciate it."

Around noon, Lance met up with Isaac Trapnell at a coffee shop downtown. It wasn't as busy as Lance had expected, since the morning crowd had cleared away and the lunch crowd was just beginning to trickle in. They both got their drinks, then took a seat at a table in the back for privacy.

Isaac Trapnell was blonde and beefy, wearing his dark blue police uniform and a wary expression. "Ryan said you needed some help?"

"Uh, yeah. Thanks for meeting me, by the way." Lance stirred some sugar into his coffee and took a sip, needing to play this right. "So, I'm not sure how much Ryan told you this morning, but you know about what happened to our dad, right? That it looked like a heart attack at first but then ended up being murder?"

Isaac winced. "Yeah, I heard about that. Sorry about your dad, man. And, um, sorry about us dropping the ball on realizing it was a homicide. I know Lori reached out a couple of times to talk to the homicide detectives, but…um…"

"No, I get it," Lance said quickly. Yeah, the police could have done more early on when Lori first had her suspicions that something was off about Gary's death, but her evidence had been pretty thin, based mostly on intuition and just knowing Gary really well. It wasn't surprising that the police hadn't taken it seriously. "But the thing is, there's a little more to what happened to my dad than just a dry cleaner with a grudge."

In truth, the man who'd killed Gary had been blackmailed into it by the mob. And when Lori had refused to accept the heart attack story and had started digging, the dry cleaner, Curtis, had started attacking her. At first, he'd hoped to scare her into silence. When she refused to back down, his attacks turned deadly, culminating in a kidnapping. Lance and Neal had rescued her, but it had turned into a shootout and Curtis hadn't made it. Before he'd died, he'd admitted what he'd done —and why. Lance, Neal, and Lori were the only ones who heard the whole story. When the police finally arrived, they'd given their statements, explaining everything Curtis had done. But they hadn't gone into the reasons why. The mafia had too many moles and it was too big a risk to share what they suspected about the suicide ring—especially when they still weren't sure who was actually killing the prisoners. For all they knew, it could be a cop.

But Ryan had vouched for Isaac. And if Lance was going to convince Isaac to go against protocol, the man deserved to know what was really going on. "While the guy who attacked my father is no longer around, we still don't know who actually ordered the hit—but we do know why. My dad was hired by Ruth Becker to dig into a strange situation where some of her clients were suddenly pleading guilty, against her advice." Ryan quickly filled Isaac in on the rest of the information they had so far. "I just need the names of the other people who were suspects in the case," he concluded.

Isaac just sighed. "Look I get that this is personal for you, but you should let us handle it. That's our job."

"It's not just about my dad now, though." Lance picked at the edge of the scarred wooden table, frowning. "Ruth Becker—the attorney who hired my dad? She's also my ex-wife. And we're pretty sure she's being targeted, too. There haven't been any attacks yet, but Ruth was followed the other day. We don't have time to wait for the police to catch up. We need to handle this now before anyone else gets hurt." Jaw tense, he glanced up and met Isaac's steady stare. "I can't risk someone trying to take her out as well. I can't lose her, okay?"

Isaac didn't respond for so long that Lance feared he was going to get up and walk out, taking any hopes of seeing those files with him. But then he exhaled slowly and his broad shoulders slumped. "I get that. I'd do anything to protect my wife too." Lance didn't correct him. "Okay. Fine. Let me know the names of Ruth's clients, and I'll send you the names of the other suspects we considered for the crimes. But that's it."

Lance couldn't contain a small smile of victory. Yes! Finally, something was going their way. "Thanks. I owe you one."

"Yes, you do," Isaac said, tossing the rest of his coffee away, untouched, then walking out of the shop.

8

____

"Tell me what you got from the police," Ruth said the following afternoon as she and Lance sat in her office. "Anything good?"

"I think so." Lance stretched out those long legs of his in front of him and Ruth did her best to concentrate on what he was saying and not how good he looked today. All rugged and ruffled from the wind outside, those faded jeans and black sweater fitting him just right. "There was a mix of people they looked into for the three crimes, but two mob guys came up more than once. The first one is a guy named Don Russo. The second one is Eric Svante. Have you heard of them?"

Ruth stopped to consider the question for a second, but finally shook her head. "Neither name rings a bell. Did you ask Lori?"

"Yeah, she ran a background check on them for me. They both have long rap sheets, and from their known associates, Lori's sure that both of them are in the mob. But they don't seem to have any association to each other that I can find. They were never charged together on any of their crimes. In fact, they have completely different criminal histories. It looks like Russo started out as a hitman before rising through

51

the ranks, but he's never been convicted—they couldn't get enough evidence on him. And Svante is a drug runner who's been arrested multiple times for assault and battery, but never for murder. Their lack of connection to each other leads me to believe that they aren't working together, so I'd say our guy is either one or the other."

"Hmm. Interesting." Ruth sat back and clutched her hands atop her stomach. "But if you're right, then we have no way of knowing which of them ordered the hits on Gary, Tony, and the others. All we have are the case files for my clients, but those won't get us far, since anyone close enough to the action to be able to actually give us information on Russo or Svante will either be too scared to talk, or way too likely to let the mafia know that we've been digging. So how do we find out which one of them is behind it all?"

They sat there for a bit, thinking about it and bouncing ideas off each other, until finally Ruth said, "Something like this suicide ring must have happened more than just three times. I'm sure other convicts had the same thing happen to them. If we can find another case, and figure out who the defense lawyer was, we might be able to get some information about who the other suspects were at the time."

"Would the lawyer share that information with you?" Lance asked. "Aren't you the competition?"

Ruth shook her head. "It's not like that. I don't do the high-ticket kind of law where there's a lot of backbiting and competition. When it comes to representing criminals on this level, I know every defense lawyer in town, and I've got good relationships with all of them. All we have to do is find a case that matches, and we'll be set."

Lance brought his chair around behind the desk to sit beside Ruth as she searched old online articles for convict obituaries, finding deaths that were attributed to mysterious heart attacks, and then checking to see if those prisoners had also pled guilty. As she typed, she did her best to ignore the heat of him near her back, the soft sound of his breath, the scent of his cologne. It was difficult, but she managed. Pregnancy hormones. That had to be it. Yep.

After about an hour of searching, she found a match. A case from a few years back. The convict in question had experienced pretty much the same thing as her clients. And the lawyer was a friend of hers.

"Bingo!" she said, smiling at Lance over her shoulder, not realizing how close he was until it was too late.

"Bingo," he whispered, his lips mere inches from hers, his minty breath fanning her face. Their gazes locked for a moment, before his flicked to her lips and back again and she swore she felt it like a physical caress. Mouth tingling, Ruth turned around fast and fumbled for her phone before she did something absurd, like kiss him silly.

"Uh, let me just call Jeff's office and see if he's in." Her fingers shook slightly as she dialed in the number for Jeff's law practice, but thankfully Lance didn't notice. At least she thought he didn't, since he was too busy scrubbing a hand over his face and standing up, putting some much-needed space between them. Because while the one-night stand between them had been nice—better than nice; fantastic, really—they shouldn't repeat that. Not with everything else going on. Right?

Right.

"Jeff Cynster's office. This is Doreen. How may I help you?"

"Hi Doreen. It's Ruth Becker, from Becker Law. Is Jeff free for a quick chat?" Her voice sounded shockingly normal, considering she was having a meltdown inside.

"I'm sorry, Ms. Becker, he's over at the courthouse this afternoon. If you hurry, you might still be able to catch him there."

"Okay. Thanks." Ruth hung up, then stood too. "Up for a little walk?"

"Definitely," Lance said. He helped her into her jacket and shrugged on his own before they headed the few short blocks to the courthouse.

It was a nice day out, sunny, if a little cold. Lots of people were out, bustling about in the busy downtown. The closer they got to the courthouse, the more people they passed who Ruth knew, mainly other attorneys hurrying from the courthouse to their offices after a hearing or vice versa. Most of them said hello, a few stopped to ask her questions about different cases or clients. Typical day.

Lance glanced over at her as they headed inside the courthouse at last. "You seem pretty popular. Well respected too, based on the number of people asking for your advice."

She snorted. "Why do you sound so surprised by that?"

"I'm not," he said, flushing slightly beneath his tan. "I just…" He gave a little shrug. "I'm just impressed, that's all."

"Good." She winked at him, trying to play it off, even though pride swelled warm inside her. They went through the metal detectors and got wanded afterward, then stopped by the information desk. "Hi, Murphy," she said to the large black bailiff behind the counter. "I'm looking for Jeff Cynster. Any idea where he might be in here?"

"Uh, last I saw him, I think he was heading for the records room," Murphy said. "Don't hold me to that, though. It's been a day."

"Understood. Thanks." She started off down one of the many hallways branching off from the marble lobby. Lance followed. "Records room is this way."

They tracked down Jeff at last about ten minutes later at a small table in a back corner of the records room, old files and dusty books stacked up in front of him. Jeff Cynster was about twenty years older than Ruth and one of the smartest men she knew. He'd been a kind of mentor to her when she'd first started, and while some people found him too abrupt, Ruth always had a soft spot for the guy.

She cleared her throat as they approached, to let Jeff know they were there.

"Hi. So sorry to interrupt—" she started, only to be cut off.

"Then why are you?" Jeff said, not looking up from his papers.

Lance's eyes widened slightly as he gave her a "whoa" look.

Ruth just grinned and persisted. "Because this is important. I wanted to ask you about a case you had a few years ago, for a Mr. Omar Butler. Your client pled guilty against your advice, then died a few weeks later in prison." Of course, the papers hadn't said anything about Butler pleading guilty against his lawyer's advice, but Jeff was too good a lawyer to have advised the man any other way. He wasn't one of those defense lawyers who was always looking to cop a plea— he fought for his clients.

Someone who didn't know Jeff well might have missed the tiny freeze in the movement of his hands before he continued riffling through the file he was working. But Ruth had known him too long. She'd seen it and she knew what it meant. Her question had hit a nerve.

Still, he tried to brush it aside. "I'm busy, Ruth. I don't have time to talk right now. Besides, that was years ago, as you said. I'm sure I don't remember anything."

Yep. Definite direct strike, nerve-wise.

Lance took her arm and tried to lead her away, but she pulled free, not giving up now. "Again, I'm sorry to interrupt your work, but this is very important. I promise."

The man's large sigh echoed off the shelves of books around them and he finally looked up at her, his glasses perched halfway down the bridge of his nose. He blinked at her several times, then said, "Fine. But only for you, Ruth." Then he glanced back at Lance and shook his head. "Who's that?"

"My ex-husband."

He paused, considering this for a second, and then shook his head. "Okay, I've decided I don't want to know," he said.

"No." She bit back a laugh. "You probably don't."

"So what's your very important question about my years-old case?"

"Do you remember if either of these men were originally suspects for Mr. Butler's crime?" She handed over the paper with the names of the two mafia men.

Jeff adjusted his glasses and scowled down at the name. "Let's see." He pulled out his cell phone and clicked a few buttons on screen, likely accessing his firm's database to pull up the case file. He did some scrolling and double-checking of the names on the paper, then said, "Yes. This one. Don Russo. Looks like he was one of the suspects before my client pled guilty." More scowling and scrolling, then, "This other man, Eric Svante. He wasn't connected to that case, but the name's familiar. I think I know his lawyer. If I've got the dates right, he'd just lost Svante's case not long before this. You'd have to double-check, but I'm pretty sure Svante was in prison at the time."

"In prison *before* Mr. Butler supposedly committed the crime?"

"Yes," Jeff agreed. "But again, you'll have to double-check me on that." She would, of course, but she already knew what she'd find. Jeff wouldn't have said it unless he was sure. The records would show that Svante was in prison when the crime was committed, meaning he had an airtight alibi.

Don Russo was their man.

By the time they left the courthouse, both Ruth and Lance were ecstatic.

"Yes! Finally, we have a name to go on," Ruth said as they crossed the street and headed back toward her firm.

"Yep." Lance slowed his longer strides to accommodate her shorter ones. He was always thoughtful that way. "Now all we have to do is connect Don Russo to the money Tony was paid and we should have enough evidence to take it to the police and know that they'll take us seriously."

"I need to get back to my office so I can start researching. I've got a couple of client appointments tomorrow to prepare for too, so…" Her words were interrupted by a loud growl from her stomach. "Oh, gosh. Sorry."

"Uh, I think we should get dinner instead. It's late anyway and you can start that other stuff in the morning." He grinned, crooking a coaxing finger her way while backing slowly down the sidewalk toward her office building. "Come on. Relax a little. Don't forget, you need to take care of yourself. You are eating for two, after all."

Ruth wanted to argue, but damn. He was right. She was starving. And while usually she'd just order something in or grab a quick bite from the vending machines down the hall from her office, today she felt like celebrating a little. "Okay. Luigi's is still down the street. Best Italian food in town. Race you to the door. Loser has to pay."

Lance chuckled and followed behind her. "I remember that place," he called after her. "It's where we went on our first anniversary."

She was sure he'd let her win, but for once, she was okay with that.

9

____

The food at Luigi's smelled just as amazing as he remembered and the ambiance hadn't changed much either. Same quiet elegance. Same small white linen covered tables. Same candlelight and intimate feel. He felt a little underdressed, but the host who'd shown them to their table in the corner hadn't batted an eye at his jeans, so Lance figured it was fine.

A waiter came and took their drinks orders, then left them to peruse their menus.

"Wow," Lance said scanning the list of options. "There's a lot to choose from here."

"It's all delicious, too," Ruth said, smiling behind her menu. "If you want suggestions, I'm happy to oblige."

"That's what she said," Lance muttered before he could stop himself. It had been a running joke when they were kids, back when they were first getting intimate and were having fun with the freedom to be a little risqué with each other. The second the words were out, Lance's eyes widened and he looked up, stunned. "Sorry. I…"

But before he could finish, Ruth had cracked up, laughing so hard her menu was bouncing up and down in her hands with her movements. Pretty soon he joined in because damn, it felt good to have that back again. The easy camaraderie. The connection. He hadn't even realized how much he'd missed that between them until now. It was something he'd never had with anyone but her.

Any residual tension left in his body fled and he relaxed into his seat. The waiter returned with their iced teas, then took their orders. Funny, but they both ended up getting the same thing. Lasagna and a side salad. Same as in the old days. Poignant nostalgia squeezed his chest, but for once, it didn't hurt. It felt like all the years and the pain and the complications between them had just slipped away.

Lance waited until the server had left after setting down their salads and a small loaf of freshly baked bread before saying, "I was impressed today."

"Yeah?" Ruth looked over at him, flicking her napkin and laying it across her lap. "By what?"

"By you." At her surprised look, he grinned. "What? It was cool seeing you in your element today at the courthouse. Schmoozing with all those people, everyone knowing your name. It was obvious the respect they have for you."

Hard to tell in the flickering candlelight, but he'd bet good money she was blushing a bit. Ruth shook her head and swallowed a bite of her salad before responding. "It wasn't anything spectacular. Just a normal day at my job."

"Well, I thought it was pretty amazing," he said, tearing off a hunk of warm bread and slathering it with fresh butter.

Yep. She was definitely blushing now. Her cheeks had taken on a rosy glow and she looked radiant. Radiant and gorgeous, and if they weren't sitting in this restaurant surrounded by people, he'd lean over and kiss her until they were both breathless and begging for more and…

Whoa, Nelly.

He swallowed hard against the lump of need in his throat. Do. Not. Go. There. Bad enough he was getting lost in the past today, imagining scenarios where they picked up their romantic relationship where they'd left off before the divorce. It wouldn't work. Couldn't work.

Could it?

While she chatted on about some of the people they'd seen in the courthouse that day, filling him in on idle gossip about them, Lance's brain churned through new possibilities. Maybe he'd been too quick to assume that they couldn't be together again. Ruth was willing to take a leap and commit to being a parent now. Maybe she was ready to fully commit to a relationship, too. One where he wouldn't have to worry about her changing her mind four years in. As for him, he was more willing to compromise than he'd been sixteen years ago. What if they were both at a point where they could find that middle ground, make it work between them?

"Anyway," she said, drawing him out of his thoughts and back to the present. "John and his husband seriously have one of the most beautiful old homes in Detroit. If you're ever around at holiday time, you should try to drive out and see it. It's like a magical kingdom or something." She had her fork in one hand, stabbing into her salad, while the other hand was fiddling with a piece of loose hair near her face. Twirling it slowly around her finger, slow and sensuous. Back when they were married, that little finger twirl was a sure sign she was in the mood for sex…

His body tightened of its own accord before he tamped that idea down fast.

No. Ignore it. Ruth probably didn't even know she was doing it.

Except now he couldn't stop thinking about it—not to mention, thinking about how gorgeous she looked and how wonderful it had been working together with her on the case today. Just like old times. And now that he'd had a reminder of how good things could be between them when they weren't at odds with each other, he kind of wanted more. A lot more.

What if having sex now led them to getting back together again? Their baby could grow up in a two-parent household. That had to be a good thing, right? And it could mean that he could once again be with the only woman who'd ever driven him out of his mind with desire. Lance shifted in his seat to accommodate his now aching hard cock. Shit. And there was no denying that he wanted her. Hell, he'd never stopped wanting her. Even when times were bad, their sexual chemistry had soared off the charts. Attraction had never been one of their problems.

His gaze locked on her twirling that hair, coiling it around her finger just like she was coiling the want inside him tighter and tighter. Did she want to be seduced? Because if so, he was certainly game.

They got through the rest of their meal, and he cleared his plate, though Lance couldn't have said under oath that he remembered what any of it tasted like. He was too wrapped up in the pounding of his blood in his veins and the spell of seduction the beautiful woman across from him was weaving.

By the time he paid the check and they walked back out to the sidewalk, the sun had set, but his desire was blazing hotter than ever. Ruth pulled her coat tighter around herself, then stood in front of him, shifting from foot to foot as if she was as hesitant to leave as he was.

"So," she said. "Thanks for dinner."

He nodded, too engrossed in staring at the plump softness of her lips to speak.

"I, uh, I guess I should, uh…" Ruth said, starting to back away toward the parking garage entrance where her car was.

"Don't go," Lance said, the words emerging rougher than he'd intended. But seriously, he was lucky to get anything out at all, seeing as how his throat had constricted with need. She looked about as stunned as he felt by his response, but she halted. He stepped forward and took her hand, drawing her nearer to him. He wasn't sure what the hell he was doing, just that it felt so right that he couldn't stop now. "Come home with me."

She looked up at him, uncertainty mixing with vulnerability in those dark eyes of hers, and before he could stop himself, he kissed her. Tentatively at first, just the brush of mouth to mouth, then deeper, his lips sliding against hers, urging her to let him in, to surrender to the awareness pulsing through the air around them.

At first, Ruth stood still, not responding for so long that Lance started to pull back, thinking he'd made a terrible mistake, but then she was on him, hot and heavy. Her arms around his neck, one leg wrapped around his waist. He thought maybe she was trying to climb him like that old oak tree they had in his backyard. Lance reveled in it, pulling her closer, one hand cupping the back of her head as his tongue tangled with hers, the sweet sharpness of the after-dinner mints they'd had flavoring their kisses.

Then the bells above Luigi's door jangled and more customers emerged.

Lance and Ruth broke apart to the clearing of throats and hushed pardons as people tried to get around them where they blocked the walkway. Lance felt like he was back in high school again and they'd got caught making out beneath the bleachers at school before the big game. He laughed and pulled Ruth close to him, shielding her from prying eyes, and she giggled against his chest. Finally, he bent and kissed the top of her head and whispered. "Back to my place?"

She pulled away slightly to look up at him with a smile. "Yes, please."

～

Talk about a replay of high school…

"We need to be quiet," he whispered to Ruth as they stood on the front porch of his dad's old house. "Ryan's in the living room watching TV. If he sees us, we'll never hear the end of it."

"Agreed." She gave him a wink and a nod. "Lead the way. I remember the drill."

He kissed her again fast, then opened the door without a sound, moving slowly and carefully to avoid alerting his younger brother to their presence. Lord knew he and Ruth had done this enough times as kids, though it had been his dad and both of his brothers he'd been dodging back then. They had it down to a science.

For some reason, sneaking around made it all seem even hotter.

They managed to get inside without Ryan noticing, then crept up the stairs, avoiding that one spot that always creaked when you stepped on it, and finally made it to Lance's room.

As soon as he got the door closed, Ruth was on him again, shoving his leather jacket off his shoulders and on to the floor. He did the same with her coat, then started on her blouse while she tugged his sweater over his head. It felt the same as before and entirely new, all at the same time.

Finally, they were both naked. Skin to glorious skin. Lance bent and picked Ruth up like she was precious and oh so breakable, carrying her to the bed as she buried her face in his throat, then deposited her gently in the middle of the mattress before stretching out beside her.

When they'd been together the last time, during their one-night stand, it had been hot and fast and needy. Neither of them had taken the time to slow down and savor the experience. But tonight, he was all about enjoying this moment and making it last as long as possible. Even though his cock was practically screaming at him to hurry up and get inside her already.

He kissed and licked every inch of her, spending time worshipping her amazing breasts with their pretty pink nipples, before nuzzling his way down to her abdomen. He pressed a kiss there as well, closing his eyes, imagining their baby inside her.

Then he continued downward, parting her thighs with his shoulders, until he reached the slick heat between her legs. She clutched at his hair as he made love to her with his mouth and fingers, coaxing one orgasm after another from her, loving the taste of her, the feel of her, the sound of her soft cries of ecstasy, muffled by her hand since they were still trying to be quiet.

At last, Ruth pulled him away and he kissed his way back up her body until he was leaning over her once more, propped on one elbow, while he smoothed the damp hair from her forehead with his other hand. She looked sated and sleepy and so beautiful it nearly hurt to look at her. Her dark gaze glowed up at him from the shadows, warm with satisfaction. She pulled him down for a kiss, then whispered, "Why are you being so careful with me tonight? Is it because I'm pregnant?"

"No." He kissed her again. "It's because of you. I want to make each moment last tonight because I'm with you."

She cupped his cheek, tears shining in her eyes, and then she pulled his mouth down to hers as she urged him atop her. "I need you inside me. Now."

Lance was all too happy to oblige. He didn't bother with a condom. There was no need. She was already pregnant and he knew they were both clean. Entering her was like heaven and hell rolled into one. The tight, wet heat of her felt amazing around him, but it was almost too much. Part of him wanted to thrust mindlessly to his completion, but the other part of him knew he needed to take his time, to make it good for both of them.

He started off slow, giving her body time to adjust to his, moving gently. Withdrawing almost to his tip before sliding back inside her again to the hilt. But then Ruth wanted more. Demanded more. She moved with him, meeting him thrust for thrust, until her legs were locked around his waist and her heels were digging into his butt. They managed to keep their moans and cries and gasps to a minimum, by some miracle, but when it became too much, Lance kissed her, keeping his mouth on hers, swallowing her cries of completion and giving his right back to her as the coiled tension inside him exploded and he came hard inside her.

Afterward, Ruth fell asleep on his shoulder, her body cuddled into his side. Fatigue tugged at him too, but Lance fought it. Instead, he stared up at the ceiling, his mind too full to sleep. A realization had struck him sometime during their lovemaking. He didn't want to just co-parent with Ruth anymore. He wanted them to get back together, to raise their child together, as a committed family. To give their baby what he'd lost.

Doubts crept in, though, like the lengthening shadows in the night. What if she walked away again, leaving him to raise their kid on his own? What if he screwed it up and drove her away?

Lance sighed and closed his eyes, trying to banish those worries, at least for now. He could think about it all in the morning. He was here tonight and Ruth was in his arms again.

Or at least she was until she stirred beside him and sat up. "Shit." She pushed her hair from her face and squinted down at the smart watch on her wrist. "I need to get home."

He scowled and sat up. "What? Why? Just stay here tonight."

"I can't," she whispered, getting out of bed to pull on her clothes. "I've got too much to do at home."

Lance sighed and got up, pulling his jeans on before walking over to take her by the shoulders. Moonlight streamed in through his window, enough that he could see her face. Hope and raw vulnerability swirled in those dark eyes of hers and tugged at his heart. He knew those emotions because the same ones were swelling inside him too. He wanted to argue, but maybe she was right. Maybe putting a bit of space between them and setting some boundaries was the best thing for now. They had a lot to think about and needed clear heads to do it.

"Fine." He let her go to find his sweater. "I'll drive you home."

10

"You don't have to come inside with me," Ruth said over her shoulder as Lance followed her down the sidewalk to the door of her townhouse. Although watching him walk toward her, all stealthy male grace and lithe beauty, was quite a sight to behold. She turned around quickly and fumbled with her keys.

Making love to him again tonight had been amazing. She'd enjoyed herself. A lot. In a way that had her wanting more—wanting the two of them to *try* for more. Like a real relationship again. But it was that very want that made her cautious. Ruth was not in the habit of making her decisions based on *want*. She made them based on logic, practicality. All of those things that were so very hard to remember when she was lying there in the dark, cuddled into the warmth of his body, his fingers threading through her hair. She needed some space and some time to get her head straight, to see if the two of them might actually be able to make this work—for real, not just in the fairy-dust fantasy world of her mind.

She found her key and went to slide it into the lock, only to freeze when she found that it was already unlocked.

Her pulse stumbled and she stepped back.

Something wasn't right here. She was certain she'd locked the door earlier that day when she'd left.

"What's wrong?" Lance asked, coming up beside her now. His lazy smile was gone, replaced by a look of fierce determination. She imagined that this was how he used to look when he was in active combat—fully focused, in mission mode. He glanced from her to the door then back again. "Someone broke in."

It wasn't a question.

Ruth nodded slowly, her heart in her throat. How could such a lovely night turn awful so fast?

He moved in front of her. "Let me take a look first. Wait in the car. Lock yourself in and have your phone at the ready. If I'm not out in five minutes, call the police and then call Ryan. Do *not* come in after me."

He waited until she was inside the car, then eased the door open slowly with his foot and reached in to flip the light switch on. From where she sat in the car, Ruth could only see a sliver of her living room through the open door—but it was enough to see the place had been trashed. Furniture flipped over, papers and books and knickknacks scattered all over the floor. She forced herself to take a breath, clutching tightly onto her phone as Lance moved deeper into her home. It was one of the hardest things she'd ever done, but she stayed in place, one hand protectively over her abdomen as she waited. It didn't seem real. The fact that someone had invaded her space, her life, like this.

A minute later, Lance came back to the car and gestured for her to let herself out. "Whoever it was, they made a mess of things—but they're gone now. It looks clear," Lance said, taking her hand and helping her out of the car. "We need to call the police."

"No." Ruth pulled away, her logical brain overriding the panic swelling inside her like a balloon. She did her best to concentrate on everything else and not the anxiety. The attorney in her knew that once the cops arrived, they'd cordon things off, and she wanted to take a look around herself first. She sidled around Lance and went into her foyer. "Let's see what they took first."

"Has this happened before?" he asked, trailing behind her. She could feel him behind her, even though they weren't touching. He was a solid wall of warm strength she was more than grateful for at that moment. "The neighborhood looks safe."

"Crime's low in this area," she said, scanning the mess of her belongings strewn across the floor. "Robberies do sometimes happen, but overall, the neighborhood is safe." Ruth looked around and spotted her TV, her laptop, and her wireless speakers all still there. She moved into her bedroom and found all her jewelry still in the box where she kept it atop her dresser. Even the petty cash she kept in her nightstand hadn't been touched. "This wasn't a robbery, though."

Lance stopped on the other side of the bed from her and frowned. "No? Are you sure?"

"I'm positive. All my valuables are still here. There had to be another reason they came to my house."

And the first one that sprang to her mind was scary as hell.

His mind seemed to be traveling along the same path, because Lance said, "You think the mob was involved? That they've stepped up beyond just following you?"

"I'm certainly starting to wonder." With a sigh, she sagged down on the edge of the bed. As a defense attorney, she was used to dealing with a certain level of security precautions. There had been some threats before—angry letters, angry phone calls. But those usually found her at her office, since she kept her home address and phone number unlisted. Having her private life invaded like this, especially with Gary's death reminding her how far these people were willing to go, was more frightening than anything she'd encountered before. She felt violated. Like there was nowhere she could be safe.

Then Lance sat down beside her and took her chilled hands in his, rubbing his thumb in small, soothing circles on her palm, grounding her again. He was safe. She could be safe with him.

"I think you should move into the house with me and Ryan," he said, his voice low and soft. "I don't like these guys threatening my family."

Ruth ignored the tiny thrill of her heart at the fact that he thought of her as family, and focused on the rest of his statement. She still needed some time and space to get her head straight without the distraction he presented. "I don't know. Let me call my friend, Collette. I can stay with her."

"No." Lance held firm. "Listen, I know you're scared. About this and about what's happening between us, but seriously. At our house you'll have the protection of not just me, but Ryan too. Two SEALs are better than one, right? And that's two hundred percent more SEAL than you'd get at your friend's place." When she didn't laugh, his smile faded. "I won't force you, but I think you'll be safest staying at the house with us, Ruth. And let me say, this isn't about sex. This is about protecting you, and our baby. I'll set you up in your own room, if that would make you feel more comfortable. Whatever you need."

She wanted to argue more, but dammit. He had a point. A couple of points, actually. And she really did feel more secure with him than anywhere else at the moment. "Okay. I'll stay with you and Ryan."

"Good." Lance stood and pulled out his phone. "Pack a bag, then, while I call the police."

The next morning, Ruth was up bright and early, preparing for a meeting with a client at work later that day. She'd gotten moved in the night before and had made herself at home in Gary's old place as best she could. Though she'd really not slept all that well last night, what with the break-in and everything, so the cup of hot tea steaming on the table beside her was all the more necessary. She wanted to focus on problems she could solve right now, to feel a sense of normalcy again. Especially after waking up in Lance's arms this morning.

He had actually offered her a room of her own, but when she'd realized it was his, and he'd then be sleeping on the couch… Yeah, no. So they'd shared a bed and it had been… nice. Better than nice. Even if it meant that yet again, she didn't have the space to process and decide what would make sense for the two of them going forward.

And speaking of the devil, Lance padded into the kitchen a short while later, yawning and stretching and looking far too adorable in his T-shirt and jeans, his hair still rumpled and a shadow of stubble on his jaw. She kept her gaze on her laptop screen and away from his tight butt. Yep. Not looking there at all.

And we're working…

"So," he said, after he'd poured himself a cup of coffee and taken a seat at the table, his bare feet brushing her stockinged ones under the table and making her shiver with awareness against her will. "About last night…"

"The break-in?" She glanced up at him.

"No. Before that."

"Oh." Back to the computer screen. Her cheeks grew warm and she squinted at the words of her brief, trying to make it look like she was super busy and not disturbed as hell by this topic of conversation.

"Well, I think we should try to put that aside for now, at least until this case is over." Maybe if he agreed, she could actually get through this without falling apart. They'd focus on the case, on facts and evidence, and by the time they'd pulled everything together to turn it over to the police, she'd be back in a rational state of mind and could make a balanced and rational decision about what she wanted with Lance. Yes, that sounded perfect, if only—

"I disagree," he said. "This is something we need to talk about right away."

That's what I was afraid of.

Lance shifted in his seat, and she scowled at him. "What? What do we have to talk about?"

"The future." He sipped his coffee. "I want you to consider the possibility of moving to DC with me. And before you throw away the idea entirely, I already checked and the DC and Michigan bar associations have reciprocity, so you'd be fine to practice law there too."

For a moment, she was too stunned to answer. He'd done his homework, which meant he'd been thinking about this for a while. This wasn't something he'd only started considering last night. And while being around him again had reminded her of many reasons why she'd fallen so hard and so fast for him in the first place, this conversation was raising some of the old red flags too. The last thing she wanted was to get into another doomed relationship with him and repeat all their old mistakes from their first marriage.

"But my whole support system is here, Lance," Ruth said, shaking her head. "My colleagues, my friends. The last thing I want to do is lose that when I'm pregnant and about to raise a child."

God, she couldn't believe that they were right back there again. This was exactly why she'd wanted more time to process. Because her stupid heart wanted to be back with him, but her logical brain was what this situation called for—and right now it was screaming that this was headed down the path to right where they'd been sixteen years ago. She felt even more overwhelmed, but Ruth wasn't a crier, and damn if she'd do it in front of Lance anyway. So she blinked hard and opened her laptop again, staring at the screen like it was the holy grail or something. "Look, I really need to get this done. I can't talk about this right now. Can we do this later, please?"

Lance sat there for a long moment, not moving or talking, just staring at her, until he finally got up and walked away, leaving Ruth sitting in the kitchen alone, feeling like her world was crumbling down around her.

11

———————

Lance walked into the new Ward Investigation offices and looked around. Neal and Lori had been putting a lot of hard work into getting the place ready to open after the agency's previous offices had been torched—and their efforts showed. They'd picked a spot on the first floor of a newly renovated building downtown, and Lance could still smell the fresh paint and floor wax in the air. Everything was clean and sparkling and new, and looked good. He spotted Neal across the large open office area and headed toward his desk.

"Hey," Neal said as he approached. "What's up?" He pointed to the files under Lance's arm. "Those for me?"

"Yeah." He handed them to his brother. "Copies of the latest info Ruth and I were able to pull together. I'm hoping you might have an idea or an angle we haven't thought of yet." He took a seat in the chair in front of Neal's desk and stifled a yawn. He hadn't been sleeping well. Not since that awkward conversation with Ruth in the kitchen about their future. That wasn't what he was here to talk about, though, so he focused on the case, which was the other reason he hadn't been sleeping much. "Now that we know that Don Russo is our guy, we've been trying to find a financial link between him and Ruth's client. Problem is that we can't trace the money."

"That's not that strange," Neal pointed out. "We both know it's not unusual for criminals to have multiple hidden bank accounts to fund their activities."

"Sure, but knowing that that's probably what happened doesn't help us actually find those hidden accounts. Financial institutions don't just hand over that information on their client. Not without a warrant. And we don't have one. So…" He scrubbed a hand over his face. "I'm not sure what to do next and I could use a fresh set of eyes on it all."

"Got it." Neal closed the files and set them on his desk, then clasped his hands atop it and gave Lance a look. "Now, you wanna tell me what else is wrong?"

Lance scrunched his nose. "What? Nothing."

Neal snorted. "Dude. You look like hell. Something is obviously up with you."

"I don't want to talk about it." Lance scowled and shifted in his seat, avoiding his brother's too-perceptive gaze. "It's nothing."

"Nothing but bullshit." Neal wasn't giving up. "Seriously. Did something happen with you and Ruth? Is everything's okay with the baby?"

Fuck. Lance winced and took a deep breath. He wasn't the sort of guy who went around whining about his personal life, but if you couldn't vent to your brother, who could you vent to? It would be nice to get some of this off his shoulders. Maybe Neal would have some insight Lance had missed. He and Lori were a great couple—he understood how to make a relationship work.

He gave a slight shrug, staring down at his hands in his lap. "I don't know. I mean, I thought Ruth and I were in a pretty good place now.

You know, since she moved into Dad's old place after the break-in at her house and we've been working on the case together and…" He stopped himself before mentioning they were sleeping together again. Neal didn't need to know that. Lance shook his head. "It's… weird. Like she's closer to me than ever, physically, but she seems to be getting farther and farther away emotionally. Makes no sense."

Neal didn't say anything, just sat back, his expression thoughtful.

Lance stood, needing to work off some of the nervous energy burning beneath his exhaustion. He raked a hand through his hair as he paced in front of his brother's desk. "I gotta say that her pulling away from me is triggering a bunch of stuff from the past—including my fears and grief over her leaving me the first time." He squeezed his eyes shut, like that might make the memories vanish, might make the constriction in his chest ease, but it didn't help. "Goddammit. I know things aren't the same now for us. I know that, Neal. I mean, we're having a kid. We're at different stages of our careers, of our lives. We can make new choices. So why does she keep pulling away again?"

His brother seemed to take that in a moment, and Lance flopped back down in his chair, frustrated as hell. "I don't understand it."

"Well," Neal steepled his fingers under his chin and tapped the tips of his index fingers against his bottom lip, mouth pursed. "Not trying to sound flippant here, but have you tried talking to her about all this?"

"Yes!" he said, a bit louder than necessary as his voice reverberated off the newly painted walls. Lance lowered his voice and tried again, calmer this time. "Yes. We talked about it just the other night."

"And?"

"And I was trying to make plans for the future, but Ruth just kept telling me she didn't want to talk about it, that we should focus on the case."

"Right." Neal nodded, then inhaled deeply, as if steeling himself. "Look, dude. I know this is difficult for you. I do. It was the same way for me. But you do know that forcing her to make plans isn't the same as you talking about your feelings, yeah?"

Lance gave his brother a pointed stare. It always came back to his fucking feelings again, didn't it?

Jesus H. Christ.

After a moment, Neal tried another route. "Okay. Fine. Forget the feelings aspect for a second. If she's not into making plans right now, maybe you can just show her that you're there for her. That you support her. And don't forget to *give her time*. I mean, she's going through a lot right now, especially after the break-in. I'm not surprised that she wants to focus on the case."

He exhaled slowly and his shoulders sagged. Neal was right. Ruth was under a lot of stress and all he could think about was himself. Shit. He needed to show her that he cared. That he was there for her no matter what. That he was committed to her and the baby. Perhaps then she'd see it, and commit to him too.

"You're right. Thanks, bro." He stood. "Appreciate the advice." He'd just choose to ignore the part about giving her time. Time wasn't what they needed—*commitment* was. He'd prove that tonight.

"No problem." Neal got up and walked him back to the door. "I'll take a look at the files and see what I can come up with. Lori's got a friend who does online security who might be able to help, but we'll need to keep it all above board and avoid cutting legal corners if we want to catch this guy and lock him up for good."

That night at dinner, Lance was ready to make his move. It was just him and Ruth, since Ryan had gone out again with friends. He'd stopped at the store on his way home from Neal's and picked up all the ingredients to make his mom's old spaghetti Bolognese recipe. Lance had spent the whole afternoon cooking, even made fresh garlic bread and everything. The whole house smelled scrumptious.

Ruth's morning sickness had seemed to be better and she kept asking him when it was going to be done. To distract her, he had her making a salad for him at the counter.

Once it was all ready, they sat down at the table and dug in. They kept the conversation light as they ate, talking about their days and what they'd worked on. She'd been doing stuff for another client at her office, and he told her about going to see Neal about the banking records.

"So yeah," Lance said, after finishing another bite of pasta. "He's going to see if they can help us out at all with that. He said Lori's got a friend in cybersecurity who might be able to give us some advice."

"Cool." Ruth nibbled on another bite of garlic bread and he ignored the gloss of butter on her lips and how he'd like to lick it off of her. Getting turned on wouldn't help anything, he reminded his twitching cock. She finished her bread and took another drink of water. "Well, thanks for cooking tonight. It was really delicious."

"You're welcome." He reached across the table and took her hand, ready to make his move. "Listen, Ruth. I've been thinking about our talk the other day."

Her expression went from relaxed to wary in about one second flat.

"Oh," she said, blinking at him.

He frowned down at their entwined fingers. "I think I have a solution to our problem."

"You do?"

Lance nodded, tracing his thumb against hers. "Yep. I've thought about this a lot and I'm willing to retire from the military and move back to Detroit so we can be together."

She didn't respond. Didn't smile, or frown, or even act surprised. Just... nothing.

That wasn't what he'd expected. Honestly, Lance had thought she'd be thrilled. He'd basically solved the exact two-city dilemma she'd mentioned before, and he'd also showed her that he was fully committed to this, to her.

Instead, she'd gone very quiet and still. When she finally spoke, her voice was so soft, he would have missed it if he wasn't paying such close attention. "Are you sure?"

"Of course I'm sure." He ducked to try and catch her gaze, to no avail, which only confused him more. Why wouldn't she look at him? "Isn't this what you wanted—now and back then, when we got divorced? For me to leave the SEALs so we could be together in the same place without you having to give up your career? I thought you'd be happier about this."

Ruth took a deep breath and met his eyes. He almost wished she hadn't. Her dark gaze sparkled with unshed tears and his heart broke a little at the sight. "I'm trying to be happy about it, Lance. Really I am. And I'm so grateful you're trying. But we both tried so hard last time too, and it wasn't enough to make things work." She shook her head and pulled her hand from his, looking away as the first tears trailed down her cheeks. He wanted to brush them away, to pull her close and tell her everything would be all right, even if it wouldn't, but something about her told him touching her now would be a mistake. "I want us both to be fulfilled in our careers. I want us both to be happy." She sniffled and glanced back at him. "You love the SEALs,

Lance. You always have. Even before you enlisted, becoming a SEAL was your dream. And now, more than two decades later? The military is your whole life. What if you give it up for me and you move back here to Detroit and you're miserable? Will you decide it's not worth it and re-enlist again? Or what if you find something else, something you love, but it means you have to live somewhere else, or travel all the time for work? Will you leave that job too, one that's perfect for you? I don't want you to do that for me. I don't want you to end up blaming me for you missing out on your dreams."

"I would never blame you, Ruth. This is my choice—and I'm fine with making it. I thought this would—"

Before he could finish that sentence, she held up a hand to stop him, her cheeks damp and her eyes red from crying. "I think we should slow down the romantic part of our relationship for now, Lance. We've got enough to think about, so let's focus on being good parents and build from there, okay? That's all I want."

Hurt didn't begin to cover what he felt at that moment. He felt shattered. Raw. Way too vulnerable for his comfort. He'd put his heart out there, and she'd rejected it. Again. He wanted to earn Ruth's trust. Wanted to earn her commitment to him, to them, but he had no idea how to make that happen. On the contrary, the only thing he seemed to know how to do was push her away.

12

———

Ruth blinked her eyes open at some point between late the previous night and early the next morning and turned her head to see the silhouette of Lance sitting on the edge of their bed. His shoulders were slumped in a way she'd never seen them before, and her heart went out to him. Last night, they'd gone to bed together, but they'd each slept on the edges of the mattress, as far from each other as they could get. The blanket didn't stretch far enough to cover them both, and she'd spent most of the night feeling cold and lonely. She imagined Lance had felt the same.

Looking at him now, it was obvious that he felt weary and hopeless about their situation. She didn't blame him. It was difficult. They both had a lot going on. Big life changes. And it was more than just the baby, too. His dad had been murdered, for Christ's sake. By the mob, who were apparently still out there killing more people by poisoning them. And now, they might be targeting her because they'd realized she was still looking into it. On top of all that, poor Lance was trying to figure out how to be a father himself. She got it. She did. And Ruth also knew that she should have responded better the previous night when he'd told her he was staying in Detroit. It would make things so much easier with the baby, and deep down, it was kind of what she'd wanted. So why did it scare her so badly?

With a sigh, Ruth rolled onto her side and propped her head on her hand. "Lance?"

Her whisper carried in the quiet gloom, and through the shadows she saw his back stiffen into its usual upright posture. He slowly glanced back at her over his shoulder and started to get up. "Sorry. Didn't mean to wake you."

"No, wait." She grabbed his arm to stop him. "You didn't wake me. Listen, I'm sorry."

He sank back down on the mattress but didn't say anything.

She took a deep breath for courage and continued, feeling exposed and vulnerable even with the dark shadows surrounding them. "I know you probably want to just put this behind us and pretend like nothing happened, but I owe you an apology. I should have reacted better last night. I apologize for that."

Still nothing.

Lance grunted. A non-committal sound which could have meant anything from 'I heard you and I accept your apology' to 'what a bunch of bullshit". He wasn't going to make this easy, and she should have expected that. Maybe she deserved it. "Please, Lance. I'm sorry for how I acted. I know it wasn't the reaction you'd hoped for. I just…"

A beat or two passed before she went on. The silence felt deafening.

Finally, he started to get up again and this time she let him go, flopping back onto her pillow and staring up at the ceiling. If he wasn't going to talk, fine. But that didn't mean he wasn't listening, so she kept on explaining. "When we were twenty-two, I would've been thrilled if you'd said you'd give up everything to be with me. You're right to think that was what I wanted to hear from you back then. But I've grown up since then. We both have." She inhaled deeply. "And I want you to know I appreciate your willingness to make huge sacrifices so that our baby can grow up with two parents in one city. I do. I never meant to make you feel I was belittling that commitment from you, or that I wasn't grateful to you for offering it. I know what a big deal that decision was for you, Lance. Huge. Life-changing. To be honest, it would help our situation a lot. Especially when the baby comes. Knowing you could be there and that help would be just a phone call away." She squeezed her eyes shut against the swell of anxiety inside her.

"But there are just too many unknowns. If you weren't a SEAL anymore, what would you be? Will you be happy with a new career? What kind of life would we have? And what would happen if we got together, living in the same city, and discovered that we couldn't make it work after all? I know things have been good between us for this little stretch of time, but you can't pretend that these are anything like normal circumstances. How sure can we be that we're right for each other after all? We never really had time to figure out how to truly be together, in the same place. If it all fell apart, after you'd uprooted your whole life for my sake, I don't know how I'd be able to stand the guilt. I want to believe in us, Lance. But I just don't feel safe jumping into things without thinking them through, considering all the angles. I'm scared of messing it up. For me, for you—and for our child."

Lance sat there for a long moment, head bent and breathing slow and deep. Ruth lived and died in those few seconds, wondering if what she'd said had been enough. Wondering if any of this would work out. Knowing there was no crystal ball to predict any of it.

Then, at last, he exhaled slowly and lay back down beside her, propping himself up on one elbow so they faced each other across the span of six inches. She could barely make out his features. In the dark, his eyes looked like sparkling obsidian, hair spiked around his head. "Thank you for saying that. It means a lot, Ruth. I know you're scared. I'm scared too." He traced a finger against the white bedsheets. She couldn't see his expression, but his tone was sincere and deeply thoughtful. "And I want you to know that I have no regrets about my offer to leave the SEALs. No regrets about what it would mean for my career or my future. None of it. You're right. I did like being out in the field with my SEAL team, working on missions. That was what I always wanted to be, and I'm glad I got a chance to have it for all those years. But that's not what I do anymore. I hate my current desk job, if you want the truth. It sucks to be bored all day, stuck behind a desk. So yeah. No regrets at all about giving that up. Especially if it means being here to support you and our child. So, if you aren't going to move to DC, then hell yes. I'm moving back here. I want to make this work, Ruth. For us and for our baby. And don't worry about the future. The future will take care of itself."

She snorted at that. "Wow. What greeting card did you get that out of?"

He chuckled, low and sexy. "I think it came from a wall calendar, actually."

"Nice."

They lay there for a while, not talking, just being together, side by side in the shadows.

Knowing the kind of man he was, knowing that he meant every word of that and that he would be there—come hell or high water—for her and their baby, filled her with a fragile hope. No one had ever promised to be there for her like that before Lance. He really was one of a kind. Her man. Her knight in shining armor. Her one true love.

She still couldn't quite trust that it would all work out. She was used to being cautious with her hope, reserved with her optimism.

Believing that things would just work themselves out went against the grain for her. But it *did* mean something, hearing him commit to being there through it all, even if things got tough. Even if her rush of pleasure was tempered by a bit of fear. Fear that they'd hurt each other again. Fear that they'd screw it up like they did before. Fear that love wouldn't be enough.

But maybe, just for now, she could put that fear aside. She smiled in the shadows, cupping his cheek tenderly. "I love you, Lance. Always have. Always will. But that doesn't mean—"

Ruth never got to finish that sentence because he kissed her then, deep and hard and thorough. When they pulled apart, they were both panting with need. For once, she just wanted to feel and be with him. So she wrapped her arms around his neck and pulled him on top of her.

He moaned low in his throat and braced himself on his forearms, looking down at her. "Does this mean we're good?"

"Oh yeah." Ruth grinned, sliding a hand down his muscled torso to the waistband of his boxers before slipping inside to stroke his rapidly hardening length. "We're better than good."

There weren't any words after that. Just touches and kisses and sighs. Lance tried to go slow, be tender and sweet with her, but that wasn't what Ruth wanted. She rolled them over again, so Lance was beneath her, and took charge. Licking her way down his body, stopping to flick his sensitive nipples with her tongue, making him squirm. The thought of having this big, powerful SEAL at her mercy only made it hotter for Ruth. She moved lower, tugging off his boxers and tossing them aside before taking him in her mouth, loving the feel of him against her tongue. Steel and velvet. Heat and salt. Hard and soft. He was too big to fit all of him in without choking, so she wrapped a hand around the base of his cock and pumped gently while she lavished attention on his tip, cupping his balls with her other hand. He was groaning low—trying to hold it in so his brother wouldn't hear down the hall—his eyes squeezed shut. One hand fisted in the sheets and the other gently resting on the back of her head, not forcing her, but guiding her to what he liked best.

"Ruth," he growled at last, pulling her up to kiss her. "If you don't stop…"

He started to roll her over onto her back, but she stopped him. She wasn't ready to give up control just yet. Instead, she placed a hand on his chest, forcing him back down, then straddled him. Inch by slow inch Ruth sank down onto his rigid length, savoring the fullness of having him inside her, stretching her, filling her so completely. Then she was riding him, driving them both higher toward satisfaction. There was nothing gentle about this lovemaking. They both seemed equally hungry, greedy almost, for the other. And possessive as fuck. Like they were scared of losing each other again.

She tossed her head back, grinding her hips down against him so that his pubic bone stroked against her most sensitive flesh, sending sparkles of ecstasy through her. Ruth gasped and Lance propped himself up on his elbows to take first one, then the other of her nipples in his mouth, his hands resting on her hips, guiding her, helping her to bring them both to the brink of orgasm, meeting her thrust for thrust.

Then, eyes squeezed shut, Ruth tumbled over the edge, nails diggings into Lance's shoulders as he rocked into her once, twice, then came hard too, their mouths locked together and their souls entwined. Nothing but light and heat and the promise of tomorrow shimmering between them.

13

─────────

The next morning, Lance was up early. He felt better than he had all week, like a huge weight had been lifted off his shoulders. And yeah, he was still buzzing from the incredible sex he and Ruth had had in the predawn hours of the morning, but it was more than that.

He finally felt like she got where he was coming from. They'd made up, really connected, and man, it felt good. So good, in fact, that he'd decided to surprise Ruth by making her pancakes for breakfast. Back in the day, they'd been her favorite, and he thought it would be a nice way to start their day together. Plus, Ryan had already left the house, mumbling something about a meeting with the old ROTC instructor at the high school who had trained all three of the Ward brothers. Apparently, he wanted to talk to Ryan about his current group of students.

So yeah. He was cooking and whistling and dreaming about what life would be like once their baby arrived. He'd just flipped another pancake when Ruth padded into the kitchen and made a beeline for the tea kettle. She'd obviously just rolled out of bed, since her hair was mussed and sticking out at odd angles, and she'd pulled on his T-shirt from yesterday. His heart squeezed with the sweetness of that.

Her scowl reminded him that morning was not her best time of day, especially now with the nausea.

"Hey there, sunshine," he said, grinning. "How'd you sleep?"

She muttered something under her breath that he didn't catch and filled the kettle with water before setting it on an open burner atop the stove beside his and turning on the flame. Then she turned and headed for the island to collapse onto a stool.

"Well, you just relax. I'm making breakfast," he continued, ignoring her lack of response.

Another grumble, then a yawn. She got up and grabbed a mug and a box of tea bags from the pantry before snatching the kettle from the burner just as it started whistling. Lance watched all this from the corner of his eye as he poured the last of his pancake batter into his pan and set the empty mixing bowl in the sink. He also had turkey bacon in the microwave and syrup warming on the back burner in a pan. Pancakes were always better with warm syrup.

Finally, Ruth had her mug of hot tea steeping in front of her and he had their food plated up and ready to serve on the island in front of them. Smiling, he grabbed a plate and glanced over at Ruth. "How many would you like?"

"Just one, to start. Thanks," she said, capable of speech now that she'd gotten some tea in her. "And thanks for making this."

"No problem. Least I can do for the mother of my son."

Ruth snorted and took the plate from him, adding a couple slices of bacon, then reaching for the butter and syrup. "You already know it's going to be a boy, huh?"

"Or a girl. I'm not picky. As long as it's healthy." He fixed his own plate of food, then took a huge bite of pancakes, the sweetness of the syrup blending perfectly with the slight saltiness of the butter, and all of it drenching the fluffy pancake dough. Perfection. Ruth was still giving him some side eye, so he couldn't help teasing her. "Been thinking of names, too."

"Oh God." She shook her head and nibbled on a piece of bacon dipped in syrup.

"I'm thinking we should go with something bold, unexpected, attention-grabbing. Like Axis." He managed to bite back a grin, barely, and keep his voice from betraying him as he revealed the first name on his list. Only the list wasn't actually "what to name our child" but rather "what names to pretend to like to drive Ruth up the wall." The names were completely, deliberately bizarre. He'd found them while searching something else on the Internet. Twenty worst baby names or some click-bait like that. Anyway, it was fun teasing her, especially when Ruth was grumpy. Plus, it distracted him from that tiny drop of syrup near the corner of her mouth that he wanted to lick off. Because if he did that, neither one of them would get anything done that day.

She paused mid-bite and gave him a look. "Axis?"

"Uh huh."

"For a boy or a girl?"

"Either. I'm not sexist."

Her gaze bored into the side of his head, chock full of nope, before she shook her head and stared down at her plate again. "Any other choices?"

"Oh, sure," he said with loads of fake enthusiasm, selling it hard. "I'm also partial to Pinches, Dangers, and Stylzes."

"Okay. Seriously. What the actual fuck, Lance?" Ruth said, swiveling on her stool to face him. "You must be joking, right? You have to be. No way am I saddling our child with a name like Pinches. What if they take it as a suggestion?"

The laughter he'd been holding in for a while nearly burst forth, but he swallowed it down hard, pushing just a little more. "Well, if you don't like any of those, I supposed we could always go with the old standard, Cletus."

"Right." She slipped off her stool, picked up the pitcher of syrup and held it over his head. Her lips were twitching, though, so he knew she was bluffing and trying as hard as he was not to laugh. "Tell me the truth or you're going to have a head full of hot sugar in a minute, buddy."

"Fine, fine," he said, chuckling and holding his hands up in surrender. "I was just kidding."

Ruth put the pitcher down, grinning and laughing too. Instead of taking her seat, though, she moved closer to him to tickle his sides, making him squirm. "What would be funnier, though, is you explaining to a teacher why our daughter named Pinches can't seem to keep her hands to herself in class."

Lance laughed and batted her hands away. He was ticklish as hell and she knew just the right spots to get him. Always had. "Stop it! Yeah, that would be funny too. Or what if we named them—"

He never got to finish that sentence, unfortunately, because her cell phone rang from where she'd left it charging on the kitchen counter. Ruth stepped away to pick it up. "It's the police," she said, then answered the call, putting it on speaker.

"Ms. Becker, this is Lieutenant Hicks with the Detroit Police Department. I'm calling to update you on the status of our investigation into the break-in at your residence. Is now a good time to talk?"

"Yes, this is fine," she said. "I'm with Lance Ward at the moment—you're on speaker, so he can hear, too."

"So far, we've ruled out robbery as the motive, as you already knew. Nothing appears to have been taken from the premises, but it does appear they were searching for something. The evidence suggests that they spent the majority of their time focused on your home office, Ms. Becker. Also, any place where you were storing paperwork and files. Those areas showed the most disturbance within the house."

"Were you able to get any prints?" Lance asked, taking mental notes.

"Unfortunately, no. Whoever did this wore gloves, and covered their shoes so that we weren't able to get usable footprints either, other than Ms. Becker's," Hicks said. "We did interview the neighbors, though, and there was a witness who saw two men dressed in dark clothing speeding away from the home shortly after the break-in. But the neighbor was too far away to get a good look at their faces. Certainly not enough to ID them."

"Dammit," Lance and Ruth said in unison.

"We'll keep investigating, though," Lieutenant Hicks assured them. "Still checking into the mob angle you both brought to our attention, and if we find anything else out, I'll let you know right away." After the break-in, they'd felt that they had to read the police in on the full situation. If the mob was already searching her home, then there was nothing to be gained by playing their cards close to the chest. The truth was already out. If there *was* a mole in the police department reporting back to Don Russo or someone else that she had been doing some digging...well, it wasn't anything that they didn't already know.

"Thanks." Lance ended the call, then looked over at Ruth. She'd gone from sunny and smiling to anxious and serious in two seconds flat. "I'm guessing the two men that neighbor saw probably worked for

Russo. That's good, though, because the cops can find the perpetrators when they catch him, right?"

"Maybe." Ruth pushed her plate away, then wrapped her arms around herself.

Shit. The morning had been going so good, too. Desperate to recapture some of the joy from earlier when they were joking about baby names and teasing each other, Lance opened up his phone again and scrolled through his texts. "Did I tell you about the message I got from Neal last night?"

Ruth shook her head, still staring down at her mug of tea, looking a bit forlorn. His first impulse was to take her into his arms and hold her close, protect her from whatever was out there that wanted to hurt her. But his brother's words about giving Ruth space kept echoing in his head. Fuck, he hated this.

"Well, listen to this. Neal was all excited about working on his first official case now that he's part of the agency. Lori was busy doing background checks for some of their existing corporate clients, so if a call came in, it was all his, she said. Neal said he was stoked when the phone rang and couldn't wait to get out of the office and back on the beat." Lance couldn't hold back a laugh, imagining his brother antsy as hell, itching to do something besides sit behind a desk all day. He knew the feeling well himself. "So, a call comes in from an insurance company, suspicious that a client of theirs was committing disability fraud to collect benefits. Neal takes the info, gets all his surveillance gear together and heads out to catch the guy. Except instead of some undercover sting operation parking in front of the guy's house, he ends up following this guy around Detroit stopping at every supercenter in town. Turns out, not only was the guy faking his injuries, he was also stealing energy drinks!" Lance laughed and Ruth gave him a small smile. "Seriously. The guy would go into the store, load up a whole cart full of expensive energy drinks, then run out of the store with the merchandise without paying." He shook his head, chuckling. "Even stranger, Neal said he followed the guy afterward and caught him reselling the stuff to another store for a profit. Said he videotaped the guy coming out with a huge wad of cash in his hand. Jesus. These people."

Ruth faked a laugh too, but he could tell her heart wasn't in it, which broke his.

He wanted nothing more than to comfort her, to reassure her that it would all be okay, somehow, some way. He'd make sure of it. But he kept his distance.

What was left of the food had gone cold now, so he stood and started to clear away the dishes. "Why don't you go and have a nice hot shower and get ready for your day. I'll take care of this here."

She gave him another wan smile, then padded back toward the bedroom, looking like the weight of the world was on her shoulders.

Man. This whole giving her space thing fucking sucked.

14

———————

Later that night, they were sitting in bed together. Ruth was still working away on her laptop, trying to finish prep on a new case, and Lance was surfing the net, looking at houses for sale around Detroit that might accommodate both of them and the baby.

He planned to sell his dad's old place as soon as they got it cleaned out. There were too many sad memories there for him and he wanted a fresh start going forward, especially if he'd be living here full time. And Ruth's townhouse was just too small to fit in a nursery and him, so yeah. They needed to find a new place.

But it already felt like Ruth was pulling away from him again, so he was hesitant to bring it up with her. She looked stressed enough with work and the baby and all. So he was doing his searches on his own, thinking maybe if he found the right place for them all, it might lessen her worries. He'd saved up quite a nice nest egg over the years from his military pay, so they could put a good down payment on a house together.

And, well, he kind of hoped that his efforts would be another sign to her of how committed he was to making this all work. And in return, he was hopeful that it would give Ruth an easy way to show him she was all in too. He'd do the research, find a couple of homes in their price range, in good neighborhoods with great schools, then present them for her approval. They could take tours, ask questions. It would be fun. No pressure. She wouldn't have to do any of the work. She'd just have to say yes, show that she was ready for them to move forward.

Wasn't like he was asking for a big romantic declaration or anything. He knew they were still working through their feelings for each other, but he didn't doubt that she cared for him just as he cared for her. It was why he was moving back here from DC, why he wanted to make a future with her and the baby. But after the way their marriage had ended, with her bailing on him, he still needed some tangible proof from her that she was as invested in making their relationship work as he was.

Beside him Ruth finally closed her laptop, then stretched and yawned before nudging him with her shoulder. "Whatcha doin'?"

"Just looking at some stuff," he said, frowning down at his screen.

"Hmm. What kind of stuff?" She leaned in closer, the sweet scent of her shampoo tickling his nose. Onscreen were photos of one of the houses he'd been looking at. Nice place, four bedrooms, two stories, recent construction, in-zone for a highly-rated school system, providing the quiet of the suburbs, with a big backyard and plenty of room to grow in, while still being close enough to the city for an easy commute. Ruth blinked at the photos a moment, then sat back. "That's nice."

"Yeah?" He hazarded a glance her way. "Could you see yourself living there?"

Her smile faltered and she sighed. "Lance, seriously. Can we not talk about this again right now? I'm exhausted and I just want to go to sleep."

"Fine." Lance held up a hand, even as his stomach sank. "I was just asking."

She shook her head and turned away to set her computer on the nightstand. "Why are you looking at listings anyway? Isn't buying a house a bit premature? We haven't even officially decided to live together. Or talked about where we stand as a couple. Don't you think that buying a house is skipping a couple of steps?" Ruth took a deep breath and closed her eyes. "How about we start with buying something smaller first. Like a car seat. We'll definitely need one of those." She met his gaze again, more animated now. "I talked to a personal injury attorney friend of mine the other day who had some definite opinions about car safety. She gave me a couple of model numbers for us to check out."

Lance nodded, but he wasn't really listening as she rattled on about what her friend had said. His brain was still stuck on the fact that she'd totally brushed off the idea of buying a house together. Forcefully shoving aside the feelings of rejection, he replayed the other things she'd said—including that they were skipping steps. That must mean that there were other steps she expected him to check off before they got to that point.

When the answer came to him, it was like one of the light-bulb moments people talk about. Of course there was a step that Ruth felt they should take before they bought a house together. He understood now. She was giving him a hint, letting him know what she really wanted.

Ruth didn't want to commit further to buying a house until they were officially engaged.

~

The next morning Lance was up early and ready to go. A man with a mission. He waited until Ruth joined him in the kitchen, then made some excuse about needing to go to the grocery store before heading out of the house. He'd already checked—the same jewelry store where he'd bought the engagement ring the first time around was still in business. And they opened early.

As he drove through the neighborhood, he couldn't help remembering the first time he'd done this, all those years ago. Back then, he'd been nervous as hell. Just starting out, with so much to prove to himself and the world. Which made this second trip a lot easier in some ways. This time his ring budget was way larger than the first time. He was also far more established in his career, meaning he had more time to devote to marriage rather than feeling the need to focus so much on his work. He'd been there, done that, and had nothing to prove to anyone anymore. Most importantly, he had so much more to offer Ruth as a partner. He was more mature, more experienced. He knew who he was and what he wanted. Before, all he'd had was his heart to give her. As offers went, his proposal had been sweet, but hadn't really offered her a lot of stability.

Combine all that with the fact that they had a baby on the way, and Ruth had a lot of reasons to say yes this time.

Instead of feeling super confident though, he was anxious.

What would she say when he got down on one knee again?

The first time he'd proposed, he'd had all the confidence in the world in himself. They'd been stupid in love with each other and stupid optimistic about the future they'd build together. Now though, life had taught him that things didn't always work out the way you planned, and the doubt crows swarmed.

What if Ruth said no?

His mind was still churning over that as he turned into the jewelry store parking lot and pulled into a spot in front of the store. Franklin Jewelers was located in a strip mall about a mile from his dad's house. It looked different than he remembered. Obviously remodeled over the years. Well, he'd changed over the decades—no reason why the store wasn't allowed to change, too. Through the front glass windows he spotted a clerk inside, fussing with things in a brightly lit display case.

Good. Okay. Time to do this thing.

After a deep breath for courage, Lance got out and headed into the store. Mr. Franklin, the owner, was nowhere to be seen, thankfully. He'd been the one to wait on Lance the first time he'd been here to shop for an engagement ring. He might not even remember Lance, but on the off chance that he did, hopefully being waited on by someone new now would avoid all sorts of awkward questions.

"Good morning," the man behind the counter said, smiling. "Welcome to Franklin Jewelers. What treasure may I help you find today?"

Lance just stared at the guy a moment, the words stuck in his throat. "Uh, yeah. Hi." His face felt hot and his tongue thick. What the hell was happening here? He coughed and tried again. "I'm looking for an engagement ring."

"Ah!" The guy clapped. "Congratulations! Well, we have a fine assortment of rings for you to choose from today. Just received a new shipment from Europe last night. All the latest designs. What style of ring best suits your beloved?"

"Oh, well..." Shit. Lance felt like an idiot and totally unprepared. Which was dumb as hell since he'd been thinking about this nonstop for what felt like forever. *Think, idiot. Think.* The first ring had been very simple—all he could afford, really. He could go for something nicer this time, something with more flair. He took another deep breath and pictured Ruth. She was stylish, understated, but with a hint of pizzazz. She liked people to notice her smarts first, before her beauty. She was guarded, but kind, with a huge heart.

The guy behind the counter must have sensed his discomfort, because he gave Lance an understanding smile. "I know it can feel over-whelming, but I'm here to help guide you through the process. Don't worry, sir. We'll find the perfect ring for your lady love."

He'd never seen the guy before in his life, but something about him helped Lance relax. Okay. This was going to be okay. "Thanks."

Lance walked over to the counter and the guy began pulling out trays of gorgeous rings with sparkling gemstones of all shapes, sizes, and colors.

"Okay. Well, first off, what stone do you like? We have diamonds, of course. Or rubies or sapphires or emeralds. Or there's combinations of them also. Do you know your beloved's birthstone?"

"Sapphire," Lance said, staring down at the deep blue stones glimmering beneath the light. "But I want a diamond." Diamonds were the hardest naturally occurring substance on earth. He wanted that durability—that certainty that this was something that would last.

"Excellent." The clerk sorted out those trays and put the others back in the case.

"Next we need to pick a cut of diamond. We have the classic round, the square princess cut, the emerald, the pear, the brilliant," the guy said, then smiled. "And my personal favourite, the cushion cut."

"Oh," Lance said, taking the cushion-cut ring the clerk handed him. It was lovely. The diamond was square shaped, but with rounded edges, all the facets twinkling up at him in rainbow prisms, from a shiny platinum band encrusted with more, smaller diamonds. "This is nice."

"Very nice," the clerk agreed. "It's one of our new arrivals. Fresh from the markets in Antwerp. The total carats on that one is 1.68."

Lance nodded. He could already picture it on Ruth's finger. The style, the size, everything was perfect for her. "How much?"

"Five thousand," the clerk said.

Whew. All right. A bit more than Lance had wanted to spend this morning, but dammit. He was going for it. Ruth was worth more than any amount of money to him and she deserved the very best.

"I'll take it," he said, handing it back to the clerk.

"Excellent, sir," the clerk said, all but beaming from behind the counter. Lance guessed the guy probably worked on commission and with a five-grand sale first thing in the morning, he'd made the guy's whole day.

He waited for the guy to wrap up his purchase, then handed him his credit card. By the time he was back in the car, his nervous energy from earlier had transformed into solid determination. Lance had the perfect ring. All he needed to figure out was the perfect time to ask Ruth to become his wife.

Again.

Not right then. No. She was already spooked from last night and the whole house-hunting thing. He wanted to give her time to relax, to realize that being with him, getting back together, wasn't as scary as she imagined. Wanted her to see that he was there for her and the baby, in whatever way she needed him to be. So he'd wait a few days, maybe make a nice meal. Then afterward, they'd talk.

He'd already vowed to relocate, to change his career and his life for her. He was ready to take whatever steps she needed to feel good about this decision, certain that they were doing this right. He wanted to build their future on a strong foundation.

Now, it was time to find out if Ruth was on the same page.

15

———————

The next morning, Ruth took her time getting ready. She had a big court case in a few days and she wanted to be as prepared as possible. Paying attention to her appearance always helped her feel like she was ready to take on anything. Even her confused and tumultuous feelings about Lance.

God, Lance.

She sighed, staring at her reflection in the mirror. She didn't know what to do about him. They'd gotten much closer since she'd been staying here. But she still wasn't sure if she was ready to take the leap into a full-fledged relationship. Her mind kept buzzing with "ifs" and "buts" that had her second-guessing how they'd ever be able to make things work. It would be a relief to go into the office today. It would give her a break from him.

She'd just leaned forward to apply some mascara when her cell phone buzzed on the counter with an incoming text. Ruth finished with the lashes on the second eye, then glanced down at it. Lance's messaged glowed cheerily up at her.

Whatcha doin'?

Getting ready for work, she typed back. She knew Lance wouldn't be happy about her going in, but dammit. He'd just have to deal with it. She still had a job and clients who needed her. Her life didn't stop just because of some mob boss coming after her.

Long seconds passed before the phone rang. It was Lance, of course.

For a second, she considered not answering, but that wouldn't help things.

"I don't think that's a good idea," Lance said. "Especially by yourself."

"I need to go in, Lance," she said, checking her makeup in the mirror again. She didn't have time for this. She appreciated his protection, but when it came to her job that was too much. "I have other clients, responsibilities. There's a big court case coming up in a few days and I need to prepare."

His aggrieved sigh echoed down the phone line. "Don't you have paralegals that can handle that part of the prep for you? Your office is a lot more public than the house is. It leaves you far too exposed."

The fact was, yeah, she had a paralegal who could do the actual paperwork, but Ruth liked to know her cases inside and out before going to court. It was what made her so good at what she did. And she didn't like the idea of letting the quality of her work suffer just because being in an office wasn't entirely, one hundred percent safe. It wasn't like she'd had any problems at the office before. Not from the mob guys, anyway. No attacks, no threats, no break-ins, even though they clearly knew where she worked, given that they'd followed Lori and Neal from her office after she'd met with them.

"I'll be fine. I'm going in."

"I'll take you, then."

No. No, no, no.

That was part of the reason she was going in. To get away from him. She didn't want to say that, though. No way did she want to go back to the old hurts and suspicions overriding everything they said and did around each other. Before she could answer, though, Lance continued.

"Or, better yet, why don't you come with me and Ryan today? We can handle the stuff at your office later, when there aren't so many people around." She could just picture his coaxing smile, could hear it in his tone, and forced down the unwanted tingle of awareness inside her. She was already far too aware of him as it was and it terrified her. He kept pushing, kept trying to get her to change her mind. Kept refusing to understand that she needed to feel in control of her choices—even a choice as simple as deciding to go into the office and get her work done. "Today we're going to try and tie Don Russo to the bribe Tony received. We're going to check with the guy's previous employers, too." Lance chuckled, the low sexy one that always got her right in the feels. "Well, the legal ones anyway. To see if any of them know which bank Tony might have used to stow the money."

It was tempting, dammit. She *did* want to know about Tony's financial channels and how Russo had been feeding her client the money.

But no. She had to get this case ready to go. "I can't. I'm sorry."

"Then please, at least say you'll work from home. I swear I'll take you into the office later. Just don't go by yourself. It's not worth the risk. Please?"

Ruth sighed. She *was* able to do most of her work from her laptop. Working from home was a legitimate option. It wasn't the one that she wanted…but she could compromise too, and accept that Lance knew better than she did about what was and wasn't safe, when there were people who were after you. She inhaled deeply and exhaled slowly, releasing the tension and resentment building inside her. Wouldn't do any good anyway. "Fine. I'll work from home. But you will take me into the office later."

"Yes, ma'am," he said, all growly and gracious, and it made her want to crawl through the phone line and kiss him silly. Not good. Not good at all. "Thank you."

"Bye." She ended the call and headed upstairs, feeling frustrated as hell with the situation. She understood the security concerns, but she needed that space, dammit. And now she wouldn't get it.

She went back to the bedroom and changed out of her work outfit and into jeans and a comfy, warm sweatshirt. Grumbling to herself, Ruth padded barefoot to the dresser to steal a pair of socks from Lance's drawer. She was searching for the gray pair she liked best when her hand brushed something hard and square in the back corner of the drawer, hidden beneath a pile of socks. Huh. That was weird.

Her frown deepened to a scowl as she moved the socks aside and peered into the corner. Then she froze, going icy cold from the top of her head to the tips of her toes with shock.

It was a box. A small, black velvet box.

The kind that held a ring.

Oh fuck.

Fingers trembling, she gingerly picked it up and brought it out of the drawer, careful, so careful. Like it was a bomb that might go off at any moment. She stumbled back until her knees hit the mattress, then collapsed down on the edge of the bed. The creak of the box as she opened the lid sounded loud in the otherwise silent house. Then all she could do was blink at the gorgeous, sparkling diamond twinkling inside.

It was exactly what she would have picked for herself.

Except she *hadn't* bought it for herself. Lance had bought it for her.

He was going to propose. Again.

Oh God.

She sat there a moment, doing her best not to freak out and failing miserably.

Then she called Collette.

"Hey, sweetie. What's up?" her best friend said.

"I'm freaking out. That's what's up," Ruth said, flopping back onto the bed, the ring box still in hand. "I just found an engagement ring that Lance bought for me."

"Oh," Collette said, muted voices in the background behind her. Then the sound of a closing door followed and Collette repeated herself. "Oh! Wow."

"Exactly." Ruth groaned and closed her eyes. It was all so confusing. Part of her was excited, thrilled even. But another part of her wanted to run away and hide and never come out again. "I don't know what to do."

"Well, first of all. Are you happy about this?" Collette asked.

"I don't know." It was an honest answer. "I haven't ever felt about any other man the way I feel about Lance. You know that. We've talked about it." She moaned and rubbed her eyes with her free hand. "But it's *Lance*. It nearly broke me to walk away from him the first time. You were there—you saw how hard it was. And now, with the baby…" She sighed. "I mean, I'm happy we get a second chance, and he loves me too and seems to trust me…"

"Seems to?" Collette's frown was evident in her tone. "You don't think he actually does?"

"Again, I don't know. That's the problem." Ruth shook her head, squinting up at the ceiling. "What if he doesn't, deep down? I keep wondering if that's why he's rushing all this. We talked about it. Just the other night, and I'd thought we'd agreed to slow down. He was looking at houses for us to buy together, for Christ's sake—and I talked him into looking at baby car seats instead. Or I thought I did." She took a deep breath and stared at the ring again. "It's just all happening so fast. And we're both under so much pressure in other areas of our lives right now. I'm just scared."

"Because of what happened before," Collette said.

"Yes. Our last marriage ended because we'd rushed into it without thinking it all through. We were both so young and so idealistic. We thought our love for each other and our willingness to do things right would just magically work out all the issues between us. Neither of us really understood the commitment we were making at the time, or the amount of compromise one of us would have to make down the road to help the other achieve their hopes and dreams. It was an either-or situation. I chose my future as a lawyer over my future as Lance's wife. I *know* it was the right decision, but it still broke my heart. And that is why I'd promised myself I'd never put myself in that kind of position again in a relationship."

Collette waited a beat or two before answering. "I'm sorry, sweetie."

"Me too." Ruth snapped the ring box closed and let her hand fall to the bed beside her. "I guess I'm just terrified of making the same mistakes again. Especially since Lance seems hellbent on rushing into all this again." Ugh. Her pulse was pounding and her head ached. She sat up, shoulders sagging. "Then there's this other little voice in my head whispering that what if this is our last chance? What if I say no this time and he's gone? Forever?"

"Hey, now," Collette said, being the voice of reason Ruth needed so much at that moment. "Listen. Just calm down. Nothing's happened yet. You still have time to sort through this, okay? Just breathe. Right now. Do it with me." They took several moments and breaths together, until Ruth's heart rate slowed and she could think clearly again, her panic reduced to a low-grade anxiety once more. "Good," Collette said finally. "Good. Now, I'm going to tell you the same thing I always do when you've got a hard choice to make. Trust your gut. It won't ever lead you wrong. Then, whatever it says, do it. Take that leap."

"I'm not sure," Ruth said. "What if I'm wrong?"

"Then you're wrong. It won't kill you. You'll make a better choice next time."

She made it all sound so simple. Maybe it was, for someone else. Ruth had been an overthinker from way back, though, and it wasn't going to stop now, no matter what her instincts said.

"Sweetie," Collette continued. "You got this. You do. If you're not ready to get married, just tell Lance that. Explain to him how you're feeling. If he truly loves you, he'll give you the time you need."

"Okay." She knew her friend was right, but deep inside, Ruth was still worried. "Thanks for talking me down off the ledge."

"What are friends for, huh?" Collette laughed. "We still on for dinner next week?"

"Maybe. I'll need to see how things go with the investigation," Ruth said, getting up and putting the ring box back where she found it. Lance would be home soon and she didn't want him to know she'd been snooping. "Until we get it wrapped up, it's safer for me not to be out and about unless I have to be. Call you later?"

"Absolutely."

They ended the call and Ruth pulled on some socks, then went downstairs to try and get some work done. They'd have to have a talk, but she wasn't ready yet. She was surprised to see Ryan in the kitchen, getting some water from the fridge. Immediately, her pulse kicked up again. She hadn't exactly been quiet on the phone with Collette. Had he heard her conversation? She swallowed hard and tried to sound as casual as possible as she walked into the living room. "Hey, Ryan. Didn't hear you come in."

He straightened and glanced out at her from across the island, his expression unreadable. "Hey. I just got here. You working from home today?"

"Yep," Ruth said, sinking down onto the sofa and grabbing her laptop from the coffee table. He didn't act like he'd heard anything, but you never knew, especially with Ryan. "I was just on the phone with a friend."

"That's nice," he said, walking past her and down the hall toward his room. "I've got some stuff to handle myself. See you in a bit."

The sounding of his door closing should have been a relief, but with all the other stress she was under, it didn't do Ruth any favors.

16

Lance was at home, making dinner for him and Ruth, when Ryan walked into the kitchen and over to his side at the stove.

"We need to talk," Ryan whispered low.

Surprised, Lance glanced over at him. He'd been waiting to hear those words from Ryan for weeks—but the timing wasn't great. "This isn't really the best time. I need to watch the food. The chicken's going to be done soon and this sauce will burn if I don't keep stirring it constantly."

"It's important," his brother said, his expression urgent.

He took a deep breath and shut off the burner under the sauce. Fine. Given Ryan's tone, maybe he was finally going to tell him why the hell he'd been on leave so long from his SEAL team and why none of the Navy brass seemed to care. He wiped his hands on a towel, then gestured for Ryan to follow him down the hall to his office for some privacy.

Once the door was closed, Lance crossed his arms, ready to hear whatever his brother had to tell him. "What's up?"

Ryan sighed, hands on hips and gaze trained on his toes. "Earlier today, I heard Ruth on the phone with her friend and she said she'd found a ring in your room and that you were going to propose."

Okay. Maybe he wasn't so ready after all.

That had not been what Lance had expected.

Heat climbing up his neck from beneath the collar of his black t-shirt, Lance ground his teeth, not sure if he was more pissed that Ruth was snooping through his drawers or that Ryan was listening in on her phone conversations.

"Is that true? Are you going to ask her to marry you?" his brother asked, eyebrows raised. "Because from what she said to her friend, that would be a huge mistake. Ruth's not ready."

Lance exhaled slowly, summoning all his inner calm. He was already nervous enough about tonight. He didn't need this extra stress adding to it. "You don't know what you're talking about." He had to believe that, had to think that Ryan had misunderstood or was just mistaken. He *needed* this. Needed to know that Ruth truly was all-in on their future, that she didn't already have one foot out the door. He needed to believe it would all work out. And this conversation was. Not. Helping.

His brother shook his head and looked away. "Dude, I heard her say those exact words."

Shit. He stalked over to the desk and began to fuss with the stuff on top of it. Papers and folders and a bunch of sticky notes he should probably throw out anyway. "She *is* ready," he protested, flinching a little at his tone of voice. Was he trying to convince Ryan or himself? "She just needs to know how committed I am to this. To her. Asking her to marry me will prove that to her once and for all. And once she's sure of us, we can figure out everything else. This is the next step. It's what makes sense."

Lance scrubbed a hand over his face, forcing his own doubts deeper. He was sure. He was. No going back now. He turned back to face Ryan, who was still looking at him with a dubious stare. He kept his voice deliberately low so Ruth wouldn't overhear them from where she was hanging out upstairs. "Look. Ruth and I still love each other. And we aren't getting any younger. We have a baby on the way. I see no reason to wait."

"Dude." The disbelief in Ryan's eyes only grew stronger. "Listen to me. I'm trying to help you here. I know you love her and she loves you too. I know about the baby, too. But you can't always control the consequences of your actions. Trust me on this. And the consequences of you proposing to her now will be bad."

No. Just…no. He wouldn't accept that.

He walked back over to the door and yanked it open, not even bothering to lower his voice now. "I don't care. If asking her to commit to me ruins our relationship, then it wasn't much of one to begin with, was it?"

Lance went back to the kitchen, angry at himself and Ryan and the whole damned situation. Dinner was nearly done and it only took a few minutes to finish the sauce and get the chicken out of the oven. He plated it, along with the grilled veggies he'd made for the side dish, then carried the plates out to the small table he'd set up on the back patio. He'd made it into what he hoped was a nice, romantic picnic with candlelight and soft music and white linen tablecloth and napkins. He'd even pulled out the good china his mom had once upon a time.

Still, deep in his gut, what Ryan had told him burned like acid. He wasn't the type of guy who doubted himself or his decisions. In the SEALs that kind of shit could get people killed. You had to make the best choices with the information you had and follow through, no matter what the consequences. He'd applied those same principles here too, because that was what he knew, what he felt comfortable with, what worked. It was too late to turn back now. At least the weather was good. Still warm. There was a nice breeze blowing through the autumn leaves and the sun was just setting, streaking the indigo sky with bright oranges and pinks and purples.

"What's going on?" Ruth said a minute later, peeking her head out the back door. "What did you do?"

"Oh." His throat constricted from the adrenaline running rampant in his system. Lance coughed and tried again, forcing a smile he hoped didn't betray his nerves. "Uh, I thought we'd have a nice dinner out here tonight, just the two of us. I made your favorite Chicken Marsala and veggies."

She didn't look as thrilled as he'd thought she would, and Ryan's words clambered into his head once more.

Ruth's not ready. I heard her say those exact words.

But Ruth wanted commitment. She'd made that clear too. This was one of the steps to get them where he wanted them to be. One of the steps that would make her feel like they were doing this right, not skipping anything. He had a plan. Stick to the plan.

In his back pocket the ring box from the jewelers felt like a grenade— and he was about to pull the pin. *Do it. Do it now.* Summoning all his formidable courage, Lance held Ruth's chair for her at the table, not missing the way she refused to look at him, then took a deep breath.

Went down on one knee and pulled the ring box from his pocket.

Years ago, he'd done the same thing. He prayed the results would be the same.

Except when she did finally meet his gaze, the sadness and solemnity there wasn't the same at all. Why did she look that way? Why wasn't she happy the way he'd hoped?

Keep going. Power through.

His mouth felt like sandpaper, and he swallowed so hard it clicked. "I love you, Ruth. I never stopped loving you, not really. I know our first time didn't work out well and we were both at fault for that. But I forgive you for your part in it and hope you'll do the same for me. I want to try again. I want to marry you and build a future with you." Hands shaking slightly, he held the ring higher, so it caught the candlelight and sent shards of rainbow light glittering off the patio. "Ruth Becker. Will you be my wife? Again."

For what felt like a small eternity, Ruth just looked at him. Then she looked at the ring, her dark eyes filling with tears. Her breath caught and his chest squeezed tight, robbing him of what little oxygen was left in his lungs. "I…" She stopped and shook her head. "I need more time, Lance. Please. I need more time to think about this."

Panic clawed inside him. No. He was losing her. Losing everything. This could not be happening. He'd done everything she wanted, everything she'd asked. Why the hell wasn't it enough? Why the hell wasn't *he* enough?

He stayed on his knees, looking up at her, as he asked, "Why? Why do you need to think, Ruth? You've known me your whole life. You know me. The good. The bad. All of it. What is there left to think about?"

Ruth threw up her hands in exasperation, her cheeks wet now with tears. It broke his already shattered heart into a million pieces. "Because you don't understand, Lance. Even after all this, you don't get it. You just said you forgive me for my part in our divorce, but I don't think you really get why I did it. And you need to if we're going to move forward."

Lance let his hands fall to his sides, the ring still clutched in his hand.

"You think you left me when I asked you for a divorce. But from my perspective you'd been gone from the moment you signed up for another tour of duty before you even asked me about it. We never even talked about that decision beforehand, Lance." She took a deep breath. "Marriage can't just be you making one bold decision after another and me having to deal with the consequences of them. That's not fair. It's not right. So, if we're even going to consider getting married again, we need to think it through completely first and we need to figure it out together. Otherwise, we'll just end up with the same old issues that broke us apart the first time." Ruth shook her head and looked away. "And I honestly don't think you've ever tried to see it from my perspective, Lance. I don't think you truly understand where I was coming from and why I had to file for divorce."

Rocking back on his heels, Lance stood at last and took a seat across from her, setting the ring box on the table between them. "I don't need to know, Ruth. That's the point I'm trying to make. That was the past. We've moved on now. We're different people. We've learned and grown. We're at a different spot in our lives now. We have a baby on the way. We'll stay together because we're a family now."

He could tell from the way she blanched that he'd stepped in it again, but he wasn't sure exactly where or how. Ruth gave a curt nod and stared down at her hands again, her cheeks pink. "Okay. First of all, if you don't see how that last sentence is wrong on so many levels…" She gave a sad little snort. "Secondly, it doesn't sound like you've heard anything I've said." She inhaled deeply, her voice cracking on the next word, "No."

It hung there, between them, like a shroud.

"No?" he asked, still trying to wrap his head around it.

Ruth shook her head and it felt like a black hole opened inside him, sucking all the joy from his life.

"No, Lance," she said again. "I'm sorry, but I can't marry you. Not right now." She sniffled and raised her head to stare up at the darkening sky. "Maybe someday, if we can fix the issues between us. But not right now. And certainly not just because a baby is coming. Having a child won't magically fix any of our problems. It's not fair to the baby or to me for you to think that."

He sat there a beat or two, feeling like the earth had dissolved under his feet. He'd been so sure this was the right thing to do. And now… nothing. His insides felt scraped raw and his chest ached with hurt at this fresh rejection. All he'd wanted was some sign from her that she was with him, that she was willing to try. But she kept backing away. Just like she had with their marriage, giving up. She said she wanted time, but Lance knew what she really wanted—a solid-gold guarantee that nothing would go wrong, that their marriage would be perfect with no problems, no fights, no resentments. And he couldn't promise that. The most he could do was promise to be there for her, and ask for the same in return. But she wasn't willing to make that leap of faith.

Lance nodded and stood, his metal chair scraping harshly on the concrete. "Fine." His voice sounded brittle and jagged to his own ears, but he forced the words out anyway. "I think we're done here. Us, our relationship—that's done. I love you, Ruth. I do. But I can't do this again, can't hold on to something when you've already decided to let go. I was ready to do this, to commit to you. But I'm not sure you'll ever get there with me."

With that, Lance turned and headed back inside. He had one foot across the threshold when she said from behind him, so quiet he barely heard, "You forgot your ring."

Fuck the ring.

Lance hung his head and swallowed those words. Anger would only make this worse. He snorted. "Keep it. It's of no use to me anymore. I'll sleep on the couch tonight."

17

———

After the disastrous proposal, Lance kept to himself mostly, focusing on the case as a distraction from his broken heart. Logically, he knew it was better to find out now that Ruth wasn't all in like he was, rather than throw away years in a relationship that was never going to work. That was what had happened last time and he should be glad he'd dodged the bullet now.

Except he didn't feel glad. Not at all.

Ruth was working at the courthouse today and Lance had driven her over. She had her big case and he'd wished her luck, despite the issues between them. Part of him had wanted to stay, but the idea had just felt too awkward, so he'd left. With all the law enforcement officers and bailiffs around, he figured she'd be safe enough until he returned to pick her up later.

He and Ryan were working together now in their dad's old living room, continuing their work on tracking down Tony's previous employers and questioning them one by one to see if any of them remembered which bank he used for his deposits. It was a long shot to begin with and grew even more frustrating when none of them remembered anything. Or, more likely, none of them were willing to share that information with Lance and Ryan.

"Fuck," Lance groaned after ending his latest call. He scrubbed a hand over his face, then let his head fall back against the cushions of the sofa and stared up at the ceiling. "Nothing. Not a goddamned thing."

Ryan finished his own call and shrugged. "Strike three for me too."

"Dammit." Lance took a deep breath and straightened. There was one more name on his list. He seriously considered not calling and just figuring out a different angle to get the info they needed, but they'd already tried that too and had hit a dead end, as far as legal options went. So he sighed and thumbed in the number off his list, then waited as the call connected.

"Trusty Towing. How can I help you?" a male voice said over the line.

"I need to speak to the manager, please." Lance held while he was transferred.

"This is Bob. I'm the day manager," another man said a minute later. "What do you need?"

"Hi, yes. My name is Lance Ward and I'm working on a case involving a former employee of your company and I was hoping you might be able to help me gather some information."

There was a beat or two of silence before Bob asked, "Who's the employee?"

"Tony Marks."

"Oh." Bob cleared his throat and the sound of movement echoed through the line, followed by the thwack of a closing door, cutting off the general buzz of a busy auto garage in the background. "Uh, do you need contact info? Sorry, I'm afraid I don't have anything current for him."

Lance glanced over at Ryan and gave a tiny nod. This was the first person either of them had talked to who even admitted to remembering Tony. He hoped to leverage that into solid intel. "No, that's not why I'm calling. It sounds like you haven't heard, so I'm sorry to say that Tony has died under suspicious circumstances. We're working hard to bring his killers to justice."

Not a total lie.

"Shit. Tony's dead?" Bob said, his tone turning agitated. "I didn't know. Fuck. That's too bad."

"Yes," Lance said, seizing the opportunity. "We're hoping you can help us by giving us information about Tony's bank accounts. Specifically, where he had his deposits made. We think there may have been suspicious payments into his accounts before he died—something that might help us track the person who killed him."

More silent seconds ticked by and Lance feared he'd scared the guy off with that last part. Then finally, Bob continued, his voice lowered now, like he was scared of being heard.

"Dammit. I told Tony not to get involved in that mob shit, but he wouldn't listen." He blew out a long breath before continuing. "Look, if that's the angle you're working, you're not looking for a bank. I remember Tony telling me once that he and some of the other guys the mob used to do their dirty work would launder their money through a local gym downtown. The Knockout. That ain't no fucking gym," Bob said, his voice edged with derision. "It's just a front for all their filthy cash."

Lance scribbled down the address Bob gave him and started to thank the guy, but was cut off.

"You didn't hear none of that shit from me, okay? I want no part of this at all." Then he hung up, leaving Lance to stare at his black phone screen a moment.

"Did you get something?" Ryan asked, peering at the post-it with the address stuck to the coffee table.

"Yeah. He said the mob uses a gym as a front to launder their money."

"Hey, that's great!" Ryan got up and wandered to the kitchen. "It's a big break."

It was.

Lance sat there, feeling… odd. His first reaction was wanting to call Ruth and let her know they'd finally gotten a major lead in the case. But no. He couldn't call her. Not now. She was in the middle of a trial and besides, it would hurt too damned much to hear her voice. Anyway, he didn't want to get too hyped up too soon about the lead. They could go to the gym and have nothing pan out. He couldn't just hope that everything would work out. Not when logic said it probably wouldn't.

He waited until his brother returned, then stood. "Let's go check it out now."

"Sounds good to me." Ryan grabbed his keys from his pocket. "I'll drive."

~

Ruth felt a surge of triumph as she walked out of the courtroom later that afternoon. She'd won her case for her client and it felt good. Amazing. The sun was out and it was warm and she leaned against the base of one of the massive stone railings to wait for Lance to pick her up. She'd gotten out earlier than expected, so he might be a while. It was fine. She didn't mind waiting. Breathing in the fresh air helped ease the pain in her heart.

She'd been right to turn down Lance's proposal. She knew that. If he'd needed an answer about marriage that quickly, then it never would have worked anyway. Besides, she'd already been there, done that.

Yet, no matter how much she might recognize those facts in her head, her heart was still broken. She missed him. Living in the same house with him, sitting next to him in the car while he drove her around, she still missed him. Especially now, since he was the person she wanted to celebrate her win with. It just wasn't the same without him there.

Her phone buzzed in her pocket and Ruth sighed and pulled it out, thinking maybe it was Lance, telling her he was running late. Except it wasn't his number on the screen. It was from FCI Milan.

Shit.

After a brief hesitation, she answered and accepted the call, then waited while she was connected. "Hello?"

"Ruth? It's Pat Brown. I found out about Tony's bribe. He hid it in a secret bank account, then wrote down the account number and stashed it away where no one would look for it."

Her pulse kicked up a notch and she scrambled in her purse for a pen and paper. "Where?"

"It's behind a loose ceiling tile in the men's bathroom of Harry's Pub," he said.

She wrote down the info, nose scrunched. "Harry's? Is that place still around? I thought it was condemned years ago."

"It's still there," Pat said. "But I think they're going to demolish it soon. Best get over there fast, before the mob finds out about the account number and goes to get it themselves."

Warning bells clanged in Ruth's head. This had *fishy* written all over it. But if Pat was telling her the truth, it could be the break they needed in the case. He'd given her good information before. Logic said she should trust his information now, especially when they were meeting with nothing but dead ends on other avenues of investigation. This could be their best shot. She had to take the chance.

"Okay. Thanks, Pat." She ended the call before he could say anything else, then immediately hit speed dial for Lance. Unfortunately, it went to voicemail. She tried again, and again. Same result.

Fuck.

Maybe he was out with Ryan investigating something in an area with no cell service. Or maybe he was on his way and couldn't talk. Whatever the reasons, she felt compelled to follow this lead. The pub, no matter how dodgy, was a public place, and within walking distance of where she was now. Even if things went south, there'd be plenty of witnesses around, right? The mob wouldn't be so brazen as to try anything there.

So, no. She needed to get to Harry's Pub ASAP.

She called Lance's number one more time, went to voicemail again, and left a message telling him where she was going and why. Then she called Collette as she walked toward the bar.

"Hey," her friend said. "How'd your case go?"

"Good. I won."

"Of course you did!" Collette cheered. "Because you're awesome."

"Thanks." Ruth chuckled and stopped at the corner for a light before crossing on green. "Listen, I'm going to investigate a lead I was just called about. Can you stay on the line with me until I'm done and safely back at the courthouse? If anything happens to me while I'm there, if the line goes dead or you hear someone say anything sketchy to me, I need you to call Ward Investigation and let them know, okay?"

"Uh, sure. I've got your back, girlfriend," Collette said. "If it's dangerous, though, maybe you should let the cops handle it. Or wait until Lance is there and can go with you."

"Can't. It's time sensitive. Besides, I'm nearly there. I'm going to put the phone in my pocket now, but I'll leave it on. Stay on the line."

"I will."

Ruth slid the device into her coat pocket, then took a deep breath before opening the door to the ramshackle establishment that was Harry's Pub. Yep. It was just as derelict as she remembered. Peeling paint on the walls, permanently sticky floor covered with God knew what, strong smell of cigarette smoke in the air. Smoking had been banned in Detroit in public spaces for years, but obviously Harry's didn't care. She kept her head down and made a beeline for the restrooms near the back, bumping into various shady looking characters along the way. She mumbled her apologies and kept on going, sticking out like a sore thumb in her pristine power suit.

Finally, she reached the men's restroom door and knocked before entering. Thankfully, it was empty. Right. Okay. Pat had said it was hidden under a loose ceiling tile. She looked up and her heart tripped. Fuck. The ceiling wasn't tile at all. Just a big expanse of tobacco- and water-stained white.

Something was wrong. Very, very wrong.

Blood pounding through her veins, she turned to the door and threw it open, only to find a wall of muscle waiting for her as two enormous men grabbed her. She fought. Harder than she'd ever fought in her life. Screamed too, but with that long hallway and the loud music playing over the jukebox in the bar, no one heard her.

Finally Ruth yelled, "Get away from me!"

Then a rag smelling of chemicals was pressed to her face and the world went dark.

18

Lance and Ryan pulled into the tiny, deserted side lot next to The Knockout Gym and exchanged a look. From the outside, he never would have known this was a gym. The exterior was depressing gray cinder block with tiny windows set high in the walls, and only a small hand-painted sign over the door to indicate the name of the business.

They went inside and things only got worse. Dim, yellowish bar bulbs hung from the ceiling amidst a maze of pipework. The air smelled of mold, and other than a few decrepit-looking machines and some cracked, aging mats on the floor, the gym was completely empty. There was a small reception desk off to the side near the entrance, and an office in the back, which Lance could see through the wall of windows facing the workout area. It was empty too.

Apparently, the only person here was the weasely-looking man behind the reception desk. Just as well, since the place would be easier to search that way. He and Ryan glanced at each other, their shared training—in childhood from their dad and in adulthood from the

SEALs—making their silent communication skills on point, as a few hand signals were all they needed to establish the plan. Lance headed for the desk while Ryan started looking around the gym area, easing his way toward the office. Lance would distract the guy up front while Ryan looked for any intel connecting the gym to the money laundering scheme. From where Lance stood, he didn't think it would be difficult to find proof. This place was obviously a front. Who the hell would want to work out in this shithole?

He kept that to himself, though, as he approached the reception desk and pasted on his best fake smile. "Hey."

The guy behind the desk set aside the video game control he'd been playing with thus far and sighed, giving Lance a flat stare. "Hey. I'm Lenny—the manager. What can I do for you?"

"I'm interested in a membership," Lance said, trying to make it sound as convincing as possible to keep Lenny's interest. From the corner of his eye, he saw Ryan slip into the darkened office. "What are your rates?"

Lenny blinked at him a second, his expression wary. "You want to work out here?"

"I do." Lance leaned his hands on the desk, pushing aside some plastic flowers in a pot and one of those cheap cardboard donation boxes. "You do sell memberships, right?"

"Uh, yeah." Lenny slid off his stool, still looking suspicious. He reached under the desk for a second and Lance's whole body tensed. Lenny didn't look like much and he was pretty sure he could take the guy, if needed, but he really did not need a shootout to complete his already craptastic day. Thankfully, Lance didn't have to worry; the guy just pulled out a laminated price sheet and plunked it down on the counter. "You can pay by the week or month or year. You get a discount on the annual subscription." At least they had that much of a cover story—though a quick glance at the sheet showed that the prices were jacked up. Not so much as to seem absurd, but enough that anyone foolish enough to wander in here, thinking it would be cheap or maybe convenient to where they lived, would decide it was worth it to search further afield. It stood to reason. If this place was a front, they'd want to keep civilians as far away from it as possible. Even the opportunity to make a few bucks off some poor schmo on a membership wouldn't be worth the risk of someone accidentally seeing something suspicious and reporting it.

"I see that." Lance glanced at the woeful gym again. Hardly one of the slick neon-colored places that advertised on TV all the time, with their rows of treadmills and a juice bar in the back. Ryan still hadn't emerged from the office, so he needed to keep Lenny distracted longer. "Do you, uh, offer classes here? What about boxing? Or martial arts?"

"Nah." Lenny shook his head. "Our members aren't into that kind of thing. This is a place for people who like to…ah…keep to themselves."

Lance didn't doubt it.

"Sorry to hear that," Lance said, wondering what the hell was taking Ryan so long in there. He was running out of shit to talk about here. "Uh, okay then. I guess I'll start with a month at a time, to be sure I like it."

The look on Lenny's face was comical. His eyes widened and his mouth gaped. "Okay. Sure. But are you really going to decide today? I mean, if you're new to the neighborhood or something and are looking for a workout place, you might want to see what else is out there, you know? Find a place with those…um…classes and shit."

Before Lance could answer, the front door crashed open and his SEAL instincts went on high alert. They'd known there was always a chance of a mob ambush, coming here, and he'd worn his gun just in case. Ryan too. In an instant, Lance's hand veered from his back pocket to his sidearm, fingers curling around the butt of his Glock, ready to aim and fire at whatever murdering mob piece of shit was behind him.

"Jesus Christ, I've been looking all over for you!" Neal said, rushing to Lance's side at the desk. "Why the hell weren't you answering your phone?"

It took Lance's brain a second to process what he was seeing. Then reality snapped back fast and he pulled his brother aside, mumbling a quick excuse to Lenny behind the counter, who looked about as shaken by the abrupt interruption as Lance was.

"What the hell are you doing here?" he whispered through gritted teeth. "How did you find us?"

"I tracked your GPS when you didn't answer," Neal said.

Lance pulled out his phone and sure enough, he had zero bars. Fuck. He glanced back at Lenny, who was futzing with the register, then over to the office, where Ryan was still hiding and searching, then back to Neal. "What's going on? I'm in the middle of something here."

"Ruth's friend Collette called the agency."

His pulse went from sixty to a million in no time flat. Something must have happened to Ruth. Over the rush of blood in his ears, he forced himself to concentrate on what Neal was saying.

"She said Ruth called her as she was leaving the courthouse and asked her to stay on the line. Said she was going to some pub nearby to pick up something. Harry's Pub. Then, while she was there, something happened. There was a struggle, and the phone was discarded, but she thinks Ruth was taken. Lori's already called the police."

Motherfuc—

"I need to go," Lance said, turning away fast and rushing toward the front door. He made it two steps before Lenny pulled a gun on them. *Seriously?*

"Stay where you are," Lenny said, his voice and his hands shaking. "I don't want to shoot anyone."

"Really?" Lance said, done with this shit.

"Wait a—" Neal said.

But Lance was done listening. The woman he loved had been kidnapped and possibly hurt. Fuck listening. He walked right over and grabbed Lenny's wrist, squeezing hard until he heard bones crack, not caring if he got shot. Hell, it had happened before, in combat, and he'd survived. He'd survive now too. He'd do whatever the hell he had to do to save Ruth and keep her safe. Lenny cried out and dropped the weapon, and Lance realized the safety was still on. Fucking amateurs. He picked up the gun Lenny had been holding, flicked off the safety and pointed it at him. "Tell me about the mob guys who come in here. Tell me where they might take a kidnapped person."

The guy began spewing information like projectile vomit. Names, places, dates. Lance glanced at Neal who pulled out a small digital recorder and began taking it all down.

His first instinct had been to rush off to the first place Lenny named, but instead he forced himself to stop. Asked himself what Ruth would do. The answer was "Get all the information. All the possible locations, then narrow it down from there." That was the smart, logical choice.

"What the fuck is happening out here?" Ryan asked, finally emerging from the office with a financial ledger in hand. "I leave you alone for fifteen minutes and—"

"They took Ruth," Lance said, narrowing his gaze on Lenny again. The guy crumpled down the wall like wet tissue paper. So much for effective security. "He gave us four possible locations where she could be."

Neal called Lori, who said the police were on their way to the gym. Neal agreed to wait there for them, while Lance and Ryan headed off toward the first, most likely location where Ruth might be held.

If anything happens to her and the baby...

No, he wouldn't let himself think about that. He *would* find her in time. He refused to accept any other option.

Ruth came back slowly to consciousness. Her eyes felt sticky and her mouth dry. She groaned and blinked her eyes open, only to find total darkness. At first, she panicked, scrambling upright. Too fast. The world went cockeyed and everything spun. She lay back down on the cold, hard ground, pressing her hot cheek against the blissfully chilled concrete beneath her, and took deep, measured breaths until things settled into place again.

Eventually she sat up again, much more carefully this time, stopping periodically to let the dizziness subside. She had no clue what they'd drugged her with to knock her out, but there was still a chemical tang on her tongue that made her gag. As her eyes adjusted to the darkness, a few details of the space began to emerge. Stuff was stacked along the walls—boxes, tools maybe, construction materials, workbenches. There was one small window, way up high, letting in a lone band of light. Dust motes danced in the beam, highlighting a drain in the floor.

A basement. She must be locked in a basement. But where? She patted her coat pockets, hoping her phone was still there, but nope. Gone.

Her head ached and her temples throbbed. Thinking was hard. So hard. But she had to try. Her hand drifted down to her abdomen. The baby. *Please God, don't let whatever they gave me hurt the baby.*

Then anger joined her bewilderment. They'd drugged a pregnant woman. Fuckers.

The squeak and scrape of a metal chair on the floor jerked her thoughts to a stop and panic rose like hot bile in her throat, choking her. *Oh God. I'm not alone.*

A figure emerged from the shadows across the space, big and bulky, dressed all in black. Another mob henchman like the ones in the bar, she assumed. He looked like two-hundred-plus pounds of solid muscle and he had a semi-automatic rifle in his hands. The guy stopped just short of the beam of light, so she couldn't see his face, just the tips of his black boots, and said, "The boss is coming to talk to you."

His tone was so textbook ominous that she would have laughed at the noir movie ridiculousness of it all. Except there was nothing funny about this situation. Nothing at all.

Normally, her instinct would have been to think through the situation first before acting. Consider all the angles, calculate the best approach. Be logical. But being logical instead of trusting her gut was what had landed her in this mess to begin with. Shit. She needed to think about this like Lance would. Do what Lance would do. And given the situation, she thought this was one of those times where he'd take a risk.

So she just nodded, then waited until the guard returned to the shadows. Eventually, she heard what sounded like footsteps on creaky stairs, the opening and closing of a door above.

Gone. He was gone. Now was her chance.

Slowly, she got to her feet, staring up at that small window. It wasn't much, but it was her only way out of here. She stacked some boxes and construction supplies underneath it, moving as quickly and quietly as she could, then climbed on top of them to reach the window. Using her coat-covered elbow, she struck the window repeatedly until she finally smashed through the glass, making a hole big enough to crawl through. Then it was a mad dash to get out before the henchman returned. Above her head, she heard the sound of footsteps rushing back to the door. Close, so close. Even with the stuff she'd piled up, Ruth had to hoist herself up to the window and shimmy through. It was a tight fit, especially while trying to avoid the sharp shards of glass still left in the frame. She managed to get her torso out and was working toward her hips when a hand grabbed her ankle from behind and pulled hard. She screamed, her hand clasping the one thing they hadn't found in her pockets because she'd hidden it in the inner, breast pocket of her coat, close to her heart—Lance's ring box. Much as she hated to part with it, Ruth knew it might be the only chance she had of leaving a clue that would let Lance know for sure that she was here. Because she knew Lance was looking for her, knew it without a moment's doubt. She just wasn't sure if he'd be able to find her down here before they killed her.

She tossed the ring box into the alley before she was dragged back inside. The henchman let her fall to the floor and it knocked the wind out of her.

Her palms hurt from the tiny cuts all over them and she was pretty sure her hip would have an enormous bruise from landing on it. None of that mattered, though, in the face of what was to come. The uncertainty was painful, even more so than the tug and pull of her hands being zip-tied behind her back by the henchman. He was grumbling about stupid women always getting into trouble and if she'd had her wits about her, she would have kicked him hard right in the nuts for that one.

But then he shoved her into a corner and stuck a gag in her mouth, then walked away, leaving her alone and scared and hurt, with only her hope that Lance would find her soon to comfort her.

19

Ryan and Lance stopped near a nondescript storage building amid a sea of warehouses in an industrial park on the edge of town. Ryan parked a ways away to hide their vehicle. Then they got out and headed back toward the address.

The place was constructed of the same cinder block the gym had been made out of, though it looked to have been kept in a bit better repair. No peeling paint here, and all the windows and doors had shiny new locks on them, at least from what Lance could see.

"Let's split up," Ryan said, pulling out his weapon and holding it at low ready. "You take the left side, I'll take the right, and we meet in the back?"

"Sounds good." Lance unholstered his Glock and walked slowly toward the left side of the storage building. The skies above were overcast and the whole industrial park was quiet. Eerily so. He kept straining his ears to try and hear anything that sounded suspicious, but… nothing. Then again, those thick concrete walls would trap just about anything inside.

Hot bile burned his throat as he pictured Ruth in there, scared and hurt, and that asshole Don Russo threatening her. His fingers tightened on his weapon and his jaw tightened as he took a last glance over at Ryan before heading down his side of the building alone.

Between structures like this, noises echoed and became distorted, making him jumpy when that was the last thing he needed to be. It started to drizzle, too, because of course it did. The shitty weather reflected his shitty mood.

This was all his fault.

If they hadn't fought, if he hadn't kept pushing Ruth to commit when she obviously wasn't ready to, if he'd just taken things slow like she wanted—like everyone had told him to—none of this would have happened. He would have been with her today, at the courthouse. She wouldn't have walked into that seedy bar alone. She wouldn't have been abducted by the mob. Instead, he'd barreled ahead, refusing to see all the flashing neon warning signs telling him he was plowing head first into a brick wall. God, he was such a fucking idiot.

Shit.

He took a deep breath, continuing on down the side of the building. Up ahead, broken glass shimmered beneath the hazy light from above. Narrowing his gaze, he inched closer, his finger on the trigger in case it was a trap. Scowling, he stopped near the shards of glass and looked at the wall. A window near the ground had been broken. Probably a basement window. His heart tripped. It could be nothing, routine vandalism. But given the upkeep on the rest of the structure here, he was pretty sure it was recent. Otherwise they would have repaired it, or at least boarded it up. And the position of the glass was odd. For it to be scattered like this, on the ground, the window must have been broken from the *inside*.

He knelt to get a closer look at the shards. Some of them had streaks of red on them. Blood. Throat constricted, he looked at the window again.

Lance straightened and looked around, listened again. There was no sign of anyone else in the area.

Then something else caught his eye, near the side of the other building next door. A small, dark shape partially in shadow. His temples throbbed as he went over to pick it up, his hand shaking as he reached down, realizing what it was.

A black velvet ring box.

Fingers trembling, he creaked open the lid to find the sparkling diamond still inside.

Ruth.

Ruth was here, or at least she had been. He prayed to God they hadn't moved her yet. Or worse…

Running to the end of the building, he caught sight of Ryan at the other corner and waved to him to come over, not wanting to alert anyone inside to their presence. When his brother joined him, he showed Ryan the ring box. Before he could say anything, though, Lance's phone buzzed in his pocket. He pulled it out to see a new text message from Neal. Apparently texts could go out, even with the crappy reception around the gym.

The police got an anonymous tip, the message read. *Said they saw a woman matching Ruth's description being taken into a warehouse.* The address Neal included after that was located on the other side of town.

It's a trap, Lance texted back. *Ruth's here, where we are.* He told Neal about the ring box. *Ryan and I are going to go in and get her*, he said.

They had no plan yet, but he'd sure as hell come up with one quick. *Let the police know and have them send back-up.*

After giving Neal the exact location info, he ran back to Ryan's side and whispered, "How do you want to do this?"

Ryan held a finger to his lips and pulled Lance by the arm back toward the broken window. They stood below it and Ryan pointed upward. "Listen."

It took a moment for the roaring in Lance's ears to die down, but eventually, he started to pick up voices. Faint at first, but then a bit louder as he concentrated. One was male, Russo he presumed. The guy was interrogating Ruth, trying to figure out what she knew. Then Ruth, basically telling the guy to go fuck himself.

God, he loved that woman!

Then the sound of a loud smack, skin on skin, followed by a low female groan. A red haze descended over Lance's vision and every muscle in his body tensed. He'd never thought he was the kind of person who would kill outside of combat, but that was changing rapidly. His inner rage must have shown on his face because next thing Lance knew, Ryan was shaking him hard.

"Dude, I know you're furious. I am too. But going in half-cocked won't help anyone, especially Ruth." He held Lance's gaze, keeping his voice calm. "Take a deep breath. Good. And another. Good. Look at me. That's it. Another breath. Good."

Slowly, his thundering pulse slowed and the red haze dissolved. He was still pissed beyond measure at Russo, but at least Lance could think rationally about the situation again. He swallowed hard, then gave a curt nod. Ryan let him go and stepped back.

"That was Neal, texting me a second ago. Someone called and gave the cops a false tip, trying to lead us away from here, but I told him we found evidence that Ruth is here. The cops are on their way. How do you want to handle this?"

Ryan glanced at the window again. "One of us needs to get in there."

Since Ryan was a bit smaller than Lance, they decided he'd be the one to go. Once in, he'd be able to text back and let Lance know what was what inside.

Lance watched his brother shimmy through the narrow, rectangular window, then waited, ears still trained on the voices inside, though they'd stopped temporarily. He wasn't sure if that was a good or a bad sign. Either way, he just prayed they weren't too late to save the love of his life.

"Tell me what you know," Don Russo said, leaning into Ruth's face. He was tall, white, dark hair. Imposing. Dressed in all black, like his henchman, but his was a suit. Tailor-made, expensive, from what Ruth could tell. A man who liked flaunting his wealth and status. His breath, however, smelled like garlic and regret. "I know you and that ex of yours have been poking your noses in where they don't belong."

She kept her mouth shut, years of legal training rising to the forefront. The less you said, the less the opposing side had to work with.

Russo took a deep breath and released it slowly, moving even closer until they were just millimeters apart. "I know the Ward brothers are involved. Tell me what I want to know or I'll make sure they all die."

Her insides were quaking and her arms ached from the awkward position they had her secured in. They'd moved her from the basement to the main level before the interrogation, duct-taping her legs to the metal chair she was sitting in so she couldn't run or kick out at them again. It hurt, and she had to pee too. But she sure as hell wasn't giving this asshole any information he could use to hurt Lance and his brothers. Nope.

Think like a witness. Think like a witness.

She had spent years prepping defense witnesses for court cases. She knew the skills to use to avoid giving away anything useful to the opposition, while still *looking* like she was cooperating. She couldn't let Russo get too angry. She'd made that mistake earlier, mouthing off just because she was so absolutely furious about the situation. All it had gotten her was a smack across the face that was loud enough to echo off the concrete walls. She couldn't keep making him angry— not if she wanted to protect herself and her baby. She needed to drag this out, give Lance time to find her. Avoidance was the name of the game.

So she needed to give Russo and his men something. Not necessarily the truth, but something that sounded like it. A misdirection. She said the first thing that came to mind. "What is it you want to know, exactly?"

The man blinked at her, his eyes cold and dark, as if he was weighing whether or not to just shoot her and be done with it. Then, finally, he dropped his hand. He fiddled with his tie and took a deep breath, giving Ruth a disgusted look like she was worse than dogshit he'd found on the bottom of his shoe, then visibly forced himself to relax, his expression going flat. "For the last time, Ms. Becker," he spat out her name like a curse, "I want to know exactly what you and your ex-husband have found while you have been digging into my business affairs. You have ten seconds to start answering or I will have Mozzie here blow your brains out."

Mozzie, the huge henchman from the basement, raised his semi-automatic and aimed the laser guide right between her eyes.

"Nine, eight…" Russo counted down unhelpfully.

Think like a witness. Think like a witness.

Okay, she'd start with the part of the story they already knew about. It was clear to her now that Pat Brown was working for the mafia—that was why he'd given her the false clue and encouraged her to check it out right away. If Pat had reported back about their conversations, that meant Russo knew she was aware that Tony had been bribed to take the fall for Russo's crime. She could work with that.

"Well, I first got suspicious when my client, Tony Marks, told me he wanted to plead guilty." Not quite true—she'd gotten suspicious with the first client who had changed his plea and then mysteriously died. But it was only with Tony that she'd decided to dig into it and investigate what was going on. Once was a fluke, twice was a coincidence—three times was a pattern. But no need to mention that if they only knew she was looking into Tony. "It just seemed so strange to me. I mean, I was sure he hadn't done it. He had an alibi. The police didn't take the alibi seriously because it seemed too cheesy—he was visiting his dying grandma? Really? Oh, and she died, so she can't verify that he was there?—but it honestly did line up with what I was told by the family about how often Tony visited once the grandmother was in hospice. But why would an innocent man want to plead guilty? Was he being threatened? Coerced? It just didn't make sense to me."

She paused there.

"And?" Russo pressed, impatiently.

"And what?" she repeated, secretly relishing the way Russo's jaw ticked with frustration.

"And what did you find out?" he spat out.

"Well, I didn't really have a chance to look into it for long before Tony died. And that seemed strange, too. He didn't have a history of heart disease. The autopsy didn't show any signs of excessive arterial sclerosis, and his blood pressure was under control." *Misdirect. Misdi-*

rect. "Not that that's necessarily the only reason for a heart attack. People overdose all the time. Sometimes it's just a matter of chance, really. I mean, just look at the Fentanyl mess right now in this country. So many people dying because of traces of it in their drugs when it shouldn't be there at all and…"

Yeah, she was rambling now. Russo's gaze, along with the guys' behind him, had taken on a slightly dazed quality. It was one of her best tricks for her clients to use in the courtroom. Lull the jury into a sense of boredom. Everyone on a jury expected court cases to be like TV—full of exciting confessions on the witness stand. If the witness instead just came across as average and uninteresting, the jury was less likely to view them as dangerous or threatening.

Of course, she was the one on the witness stand right now—and with her hands bound behind her back, she was the *essence* of unthreatening. Meanwhile, the men with guns in front of her were the opposite.

Please God, let Lance get here quickly. Please.

"Stop!" Russo said, loud and deep, enough to make Ruth jump. "Stop with the bullshit. No more stalling." He gestured to Mozzie again and there went that laser dot, right between her eyes for the second time. There was no way she could actually feel it, but Ruth swore it burned her skin there. "Tell me what I want to know now, facts only, or you die and I toss your body in the river, where it'll take them days to find it. The fish there do love their meals."

Ruth shuddered. Couldn't help it. The thought of her baby becoming fish food made her want to puke.

"Seven, six…" Russo continued his countdown and Ruth's prospects of being rescued grew dim.

20

"He's too close," Lance whispered to Ryan from behind a tall stack of crates they were hiding behind. Ryan had silently let him in through a side door a few minutes prior and they'd been scoping out Russo and his goons, trying to figure out the best plan of attack. There were four opponents and only two Ward brothers at present. Not the best odds, especially since Russo's guys were heavily armed. Lance cursed under his breath. "Russo's at the wrong angle."

"Mozzie, come here," Russo yelled and the bulky guy on the left stepped forward, AR-15 in one hand, pointed at Ruth. Lance fisted his hands so hard at his sides, his bones cracked. He wished they were around that fucker's throat. Russo waggled his fingers at the henchman, his gaze trained on Ruth. "Give me your knife."

Just a little more. Just a little more.

Lance raised his Glock and aimed at the henchman's legs. He gave his brother a quick glance to let him know what was going down and Ryan nodded, scurrying past him to another set of crates across the aisle, sticking to the shadows and moving noiselessly, to avoid detection while he got into position.

Ruth was staring up at Russo, her face pale and bruised on one side, a tiny trickle of blood coming from the corner of her mouth. Her dark eyes flashed with a volatile mix of hatred and horror. Lance's chest squeezed tight as he promised himself that he'd avenge every second of pain and fear she'd experienced.

The guard took another step toward Russo and Lance fired, hitting the big guy in the back of the thigh. He went down hard. At the same time, Ryan fired at another henchman, hitting him in the shoulder. Chaos ensued. The two other bodyguards with Russo turned and began shooting into the shadows where the shots had come from, but Lance and Ryan had anticipated that and were already on the move, rushing forward to take down the additional guards by tackling them and knocking them to the ground.

Lance turned just in time to avoid being stabbed in the head by the fucker's blade, but dropped his Glock in the process. Shit. He scrambled on the ground for another weapon, one of the ones he'd kicked aside from the guards earlier during his and Ryan's surprise attack.

Russo's attention was zeroed on him as he moved forward with murderous intent, knife gripped tight and raised to strike. The only good thing about that was that it meant he didn't see Ruth behind him, still tied to the chair but determined to lash out at her kidnapper. The metal legs of her chair scraped loudly against the concrete floor as she rocked herself close to Russo, but he didn't seem to notice until it was too late. Ruth pitched back hard, then forward again, toppling herself into Russo and knocking him off balance. He tripped toward Lance and fell to the ground.

Lance didn't waste any time, launching himself onto the fucker and pummelling him for all he was worth. He was vaguely aware of Ryan battling the other two guards, but he seemed to be holding his own just fine. They trained 'em tough in the SEALs.

Russo, however, wasn't going down without a fight and Lance was more than willing to give him one. They tumbled across the hard concrete floor, Lance landing several hard blows to the man's ribs and stomach, even as the fingers around his throat tightened. He felt bone give way under his fist and from Russo's pained grunt, he'd broken a couple of ribs. Good. The red haze descended again over Lance's vision. Everything became hyper-real—the damp chill in the air, the cold hard floor beneath him, the smell of sweat and desperation reeking off Russo. Lance went into full SEAL mode, where there was only the now, only the mission, only one objective. Take this fucker down. Now.

He kicked, punched, jerked his body hard right and left in an attempt to dislodge his opponent.

Finally, he managed to jam his knee into Russo's crotch. The man's expression turned almost comical for a second, eyes round and mouth gaping, only a short squeak of agony escaping before he toppled over on the ground holding himself.

Dirty fighting? Maybe. But all was fair in love and war—and this was both.

While Lance scrambled away, Ryan finished taking down the other two guards and secured them, then ran over and kicked Russo hard in the back before yanking his arms behind his back and zip-tying them at the wrists. "That was for my dad, motherfucker."

Normal breathing restored and red receding from his peripheral vision, Lance pushed to his feet and ran for Ruth. She was still secured to her chair and cursing a blue streak as she lay on her side on the floor. Lance righted her chair, then pulled out his collapsible knife from his back pocket and made quick work of the zip ties binding her hands before kneeling at her feet to slice through the tape. Then she was on the floor in front of him, on her knees. Ruth was in his arms, holding him tight, and nothing else mattered. Not the criminals on the floor behind him, not the painful burn in his throat from being choked. Not anything.

Just the fact that Ruth was safe. Their baby was safe. At least he thought so…

He pulled back, cupping her bruised face carefully to make her look at him. "Are you okay? You're bleeding." He swiped the trickle of blood away from the corner of her mouth. "They didn't hurt you anywhere else, did they? The baby. Did they…"

Ruth shook her head. "They drugged me to knock me out—I'll need to ask the EMT if that could harm the baby. But other than that, I'm fine. The worst I got was a slap across the face. So glad you showed up when you did, though, because Russo was about to rearrange my face, and not in a Beverly Hills plastic surgeon kind of way."

"Oh God." Lance pulled her to him again, hugging her tight. He needed that connection, that solid feel of her in his arms, the steady thud of her heartbeat next to his. Eyes squeezed shut, the guilt and fear washed over him at last, making him babble like an idiot. "I'm sorry, Ruth. I'm so, so sorry. I should've been there with you, at the courthouse, no matter how awkward it was. If I'd been there, none of this would've happened. It's all my fault. But I swear to you, I'll always have your back from here on out. Regardless of what's going on with us, whether you love me anymore or not. I'll never let anything like this ever happen to you again. I swear on my life."

Outside the building, the screech of tires heralded the arrived of the police. Soon the place was swarming with cops, seizing the weapons scattered on the floor and taking the henchmen into custody.

Behind them, Russo scrabbled and shouted as the cops came for him too. "I want my attorney. I have rights."

Ruth looked over at him again, her expression disgusted. "No attorney in the world can save you, asshole. You're going down."

"Jesus," Neal said, crouching down beside Lance. "You guys okay? Looks like a war zone in here."

"I'm okay," he said, then hiked his chin toward Ruth. "I want her checked at the hospital, though. I want everything documented and I want the baby checked as well. If they find anything wrong, I'm going after Russo myself, rights or not."

Neal straightened and helped them up. "There's an ambulance on the way."

The next half hour or so passed in a blur. The cops took their initial statements, then released them to the EMTs, who'd arrived to take Ruth to the hospital. The ride there was rough, with Lance holding her hand the whole time, afraid to let her go for fear he'd lose her all over again.

Finally they were in the ER and she was checked over by a doctor before being hooked up to a fetal monitor. It was still early in the pregnancy, but thankfully the baby's heartbeat was sure and strong. For the first time since the nightmare began, Lance believed Ruth and the baby were okay.

After the rush and roar of the crime scene, it was just the two of them at last. Well, three, if you counted the baby, which Lance did. He still had a hold of Ruth's hand. The nurse had pulled the curtain around Ruth's area, giving them some privacy, and an air of intimacy settled, the regular thump of the baby's pulse drowning out the hubbub outside.

With his free hand, Lance reached into his pocket and pulled out the ring box. He set it on the side of her bed, then stared at it as he said, "I wanted to give this back to you. Great clue, by the way." He gave a sad little snort. "Anyway, I know I was trying to rush you because of my own insecurities, but today made me realize that I don't work without you, Ruth. Nothing in my life makes sense without you in it."

This was hard, so hard. And scary. Way scarier than staring down the barrel of a sniper's gun or facing down Don Russo and his knife earlier. But he took a deep breath and continued, summoning all his SEAL courage. "I want a relationship that lasts, Ruth. With you. And I want it to be good for both of us. So, I'm willing to take it slow. As slow as you need. If you're still willing to have me."

Her quiet gasp made him look up, to see tears sparkling in her gorgeous eyes. She was smiling at him and beckoning him closer with her free hand. When he leaned in, she kissed him, slow and soft and sweet. "God, I love you, Lance Ward. I really, really do. I want to keep saying it, every day, for the rest of my life."

Joy swelled inside him like a balloon, pushing away all the doubts and darkness. He smiled down at her. "You know, today I found you in time and got you out safely because I started to think like you. I got all the information first, then I waited for the right time."

She laughed, the sound chiming around him like rainbow prisms. "The reason I threw the ring box out the window was because I was thinking like you, Lance. I thought, 'What would Lance do right now?' I knew the answer was 'Act boldly and on pure instinct.' So that's what I did, too."

They kissed again. Then Lance pulled his chair closer and took a seat, still holding her hand.

Ruth sighed and placed her free hand over her abdomen. "Sitting in that dank basement, waiting for Russo to show up, I finally saw that I might have been wrong about our first marriage," she said, and his breath caught in his throat. "I realize now that the problem wasn't that we went into it without having everything figured out. The problem was that as we figured things out, we grew apart. And rather than trying to fix that, I gave up." She frowned and shook her head, gripping his hand tighter. "But that won't happen again. This time we can grow together, Lance. We're already doing that. Figuring out how to be a better couple as we go."

He watched as she let him go to pick up the ring box. Ruth opened it and took out the ring, then slid it onto her finger. It sparkled like a new-born day under the overhead lights. Lance swallowed hard, his throat aching. Whether from the choking or from emotion, he didn't want to say.

"I'm ready to take the leap," Ruth said, her voice rough with happy tears. "You're right, Lance. Sometimes you need to take a big risk, because you know in your gut it's the right thing to do. And marrying you seems like the rightest thing in the universe."

He kissed her then. Again. Longer and deeper this time, putting all the feelings he had inside into that moment—love and joy and relief and gratitude, so much gratitude. By the time he pulled back, they were both breathless.

She grinned at him. "I want a longer engagement, though. No way could I handle planning a wedding and having a baby at the same time. Not with my workload. And I'd rather we keep my townhouse and just remodel it rather than searching for a new place in this crazy market. We'll have more than enough work to do on it to keep us busy, deciding what to keep and what to change." She brought his hand to her mouth and kissed the back of it, her eyes glowing with affection. "But no matter what, I want you, Lance. You're it for me. You'll always be my one and only. Always."

His heart felt like it would burst from happiness. He kissed her hand too, then leaned over her, their faces only an inch apart, so she could have no doubt of the love in his eyes. "You are the love of my life, Ruth Becker. Always have been. Always will be. Always."

EPILOGUE

The following weekend, the whole gang was at Ruth's house, helping her get the spare bedroom ready for the baby. Well, the whole gang with the exception of Lance, since he'd gone back to DC to officially end his commitment to the navy. Neal and Ryan were both at Ruth's house, though, as were Lori and Collette.

Ruth appreciated the help, but still felt cautious. She wasn't used to other people helping her organize her stuff, and didn't really know how to feel about that.

"Hey," Neal called, holding up a bright, sunny yellow paint chip. "What about this color for the nursery?"

"Uh, no." Ruth snorted. "Poor kid would need shades just to go in their room. I want something more sedate and neutral, please."

Neal huffed out a breath and went back to sorting through his paint chips.

"I have an announcement to make," Ryan said, setting the box of stuff he was carrying on the floor. All eyes turned to him. "I'm not going back to my SEAL team."

"Wait, seriously? Since when? And *why*?" Neal asked.

Ryan gave his brother a look and continued. "There's one piece left of Dad's murder still unsolved, and I intend to solve it. That means this is where I need to be right now. Once the case is closed, I'll figure out next steps, but for now, resolving this is going to be my job."

"Well, go on, then," Collette said, sounding curious. "What's the missing piece?"

"Who drugged Tony Marks?" Ryan asked, simple and direct. "Russo was the one who ordered it to happen, but he couldn't have just walked into the prison and done it himself."

"Was it Pat Brown, maybe?" Ruth suggested.

Ryan shook his head. "Doubtful, unless he was cellmate to the other prisoners with 'heart attacks,' too. And someone still would have needed to sneak the drug into the prison. There's another person involved in all of this, and he or she is walking around free right now after killing all those people. That's what I intend to fix. Then we can finally put Dad's case to rest."

"Hmm." Ruth nodded. "Well, good luck with that. I've been wondering the same thing myself the past few days."

"Yeah, buddy," Neal said, coming up to them and slapping Ryan on the shoulder. "Glad to hear you've got something going on. Though I have to say I'm still curious as hell as to why you're leaving your SEAL team."

"Honey," Lori called from nearby. "Leave the poor guy alone. Come help me carry these boxes into the nursery."

Reluctantly, Neal turned and went to help her. Ryan picked up his box again and headed down the hall. Ruth sat there, watching everyone, her chest aching slightly. Even though he'd only been gone a few days, she missed Lance something fierce. She wished he was here with the rest of them today, laughing and eating and joking around. He loved these kinds of get-togethers with family and friends.

He loved his friends and family, period.

Then, startling her out of her thoughts, there was a knock on the door. Ruth tensed, more out of habit from the last few weeks than anything else.

Silly. She was being silly. Russo was locked away and the rest of the mob had no reason to target them. Russo wasn't high up enough to be avenged. It was probably just the mailman or a delivery guy with one of the things she'd ordered online for the baby's room. While everyone else was busy cleaning and sorting things, Ruth got up and wandered to the door. When she peeked through the peephole, her breath caught. She looked again, then opened the door fast, in case he disappeared.

Lance. He was there. On her porch. Right now.

For a second, she was too stunned to do anything but blink at him. Then her attorney skills kicked in and she asked, "What are you doing here?"

Get the facts, ma'am. Just the facts.

Except there was no way she could just stick to logic and facts where Lance was concerned. Not with her heart in her throat and her pulse racing and her blood singing and…

Before he could answer, she was in his arms, burying her face in his neck and inhaling his good Lance smell. Damn. She'd missed him so much.

He chuckled, picking her up around the waist and stepping inside with her pressed against him, then closing the door behind him to keep the cold out. After that, he set her down and kissed her sweetly.

"Look who's here!" Ryan said, returning to the living room. "What the hell, bro? Thought you were back in DC this week."

"I decided to commute," Lance said, still looking down into Ruth's eyes, his own gaze shining with love. Then he moved her to his side and smiled at his brother. "Flying back and forth isn't that big a deal, only like an hour and half each way, and I have a lot of frequent flyer miles to use up anyway, unless I can hitch a ride on a military cargo plane, and then it's free, so… I figure it's just for a couple of months until I'm fully retired, and that way I can be here with Ruth every weekend."

He gave her a comforting squeeze, and she looped her arms around his waist and squeezed him right back, resting her head on his chest. She'd never been one of those clingy women. Still wasn't. But there was something about Lance that made her want to depend on him, confide in him, rely on him.

Love. It was love. Just that simply and that pure and that true.

Love made all the difference.

Lance kissed the top of her head and she looked up at him.

"It's okay with you, right?" he asked her quietly, so no one else could hear. "Me coming back?"

"Of course it's all right." She smiled. "This is your home now."

His smile was like a ray of light though the storm, breathtakingly gorgeous. "Yes, it is. My home's with you, wherever that may be. No more living in our own separate worlds like we did in our first marriage. This time, we're a true team." He kissed her again, a bit more passionately this time, then whispered, "Also, I really missed having sex with you, so…"

She giggled and pulled back to slap his arm playfully as wolf whistles, and shouts for them to get a room, echoed from the peanut gallery.

Heat prickled Ruth's cheeks, but she refused to be embarrassed. She loved Lance more than she loved life itself and she didn't care who knew it.

"Dude," Neal said, laughing and coming over to give his brother a hug. "Leave it to you to overcompensate."

"What the hell are you talking about?" Lance said, stepping back to slip his arm around Ruth's waist again. She did the same with him just because it felt so good to touch him, to be together again.

"You just had to travel here? You couldn't video chat like a normal person?"

Ruth snorted, getting in on the teasing. "He's right, you know. You didn't even text to let me know you were on the way."

"Right?" Ryan said as he joined them. "Like he just has to make us all look bad, always going the extra mile with some grand, sweeping gesture, showing up here, surprising Ruth, saying he'll keep doing it until the DC job is done. Thanks for setting the bar way too high for the rest of us."

The Ward brothers ribbed each other a while longer, joking around and chatting, and setting up a time to meet the next day to discuss Ryan's plans to move forward with the last phase of the case.

Ruth stayed by Lance's side. Ryan and Neal were both right, she realized. Lance had gone all in today, same as he always did. Except now, he was putting that determination and commitment toward her and their future. It made the small, vulnerable part of her inside finally relax and unfurl. She'd been carrying that burden of anxiety and distrust for so long that it was a relief to let it go now.

Because of Lance. Because of his willingness to meet her in the middle, to build a life together that worked for both of them. She realized that for the first time, she one-hundred-percent believed that this time their marriage would work. This time it would really be different. Because they were different.

Eventually, the house cleared as people left to do other things, leaving just her and Lance alone. It was still early evening, but the sun had set. Lance went around turning off the lights while Ruth finished putting away all the snacks and food trays she'd had out for her guests. Then Lance came up behind her and slipped his arms around her waist, his hands resting protectively over her barely-there baby bump.

"Happy?" he asked.

"Completely," she said, turning to put her arms around his neck and kiss him. He wasn't the only one who'd missed the sex.

Lance chuckled low in his throat, sending rumbles of desire through her, before sweeping Ruth up in his arms and carrying her toward the bedroom. She nibbled his jaw and grinned, knowing this was just the first night of the rest of their lives together.

END OF SEAL'S PREGNANT EX-WIFE
WARD INVESTIGATION BOOK TWO

SEAL's Pretend Girlfriend, March 24, 2022

SEAL's Pregnant Ex-Wife, March 31, 2022

SEAL's Fake Relationship, April 7, 2022

PS: Do you love hot-blooded SEALs? Then keep reading for exclusive extracts from **SEAL's Fake Relationship, His Stubborn Lover** and **The SEAL's Surprise Son.**

THANK YOU!

Thank you so much for purchasing my book. It's hard for me to put into words how much I appreciate my readers. If you enjoyed this book, please remember to leave a review. Reviews are crucial for an author's success and I would greatly appreciate it if you took the time to review the book. I love hearing from you!

You can connect with me on:

goodreads.com/leslienorth

bookbub.com/authors/leslie-north

facebook.com/leslienorthbooks

x.com/leslienorthbook

ABOUT LESLIE

Leslie North is the USA Today Bestselling pen name for a critically-acclaimed author of women's contemporary romance and fiction. The anonymity gives her the perfect opportunity to paint with her full artistic palette, especially in the romance and erotic fantasy genres.

Find your next Leslie North book visit LeslieNorthBooks.com or choose:

BY TROPE

BY HERO

PS: Want sneak peeks, giveaways, ARC offers, fun extras and plenty of pictures of bad boys? Join my Facebook group, Leslie's Lovelies!

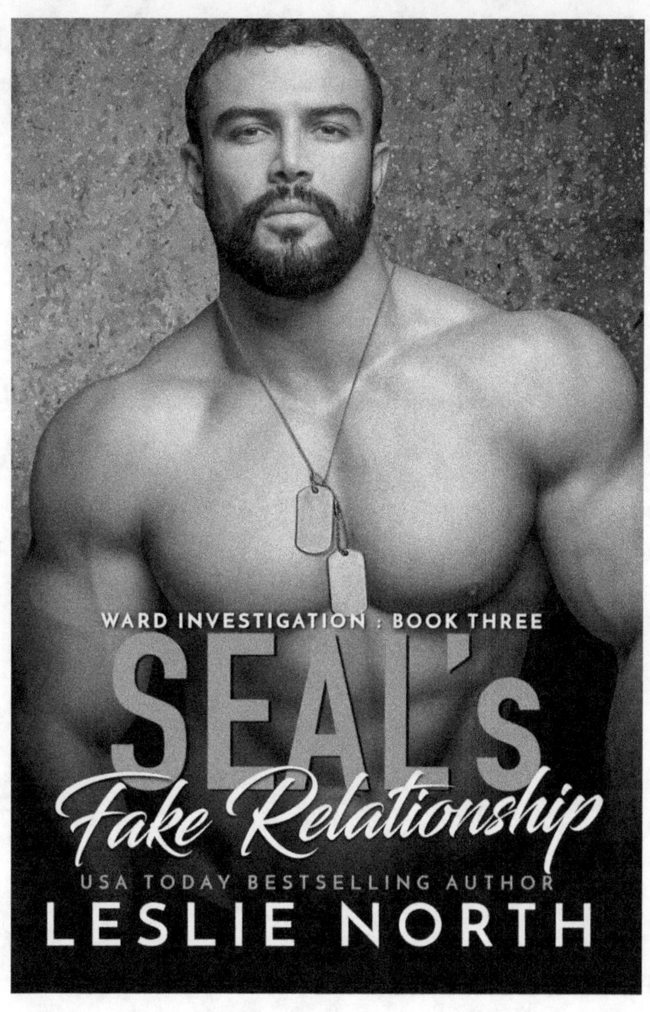

BLURB

An old rivalry blooms into passion for a Navy SEAL and his fake girlfriend…

US Marshal Kelsey Poppins has an axe to grind. She's determined to prove her co-worker is innocent. But her old high school rival, Navy SEAL Ryan Ward, isn't convinced. His father died investigating a sinister crime ring. And he's convinced Kelsey's friend is involved…

But when they both sneak into a Federal building and find incriminating evidence within, her boss catches them in the act. Needing an excuse to explain his presence, Ryan leaves Kelsey weak-kneed with the *hottest* kiss she's ever had. Now, they're faking a relationship as they work together to solve a string of murders. All while trying to stay alive… And out of each other's arms.

Ryan won't allow one more person to die. Not on his watch, and definitely not Kelsey. Maybe it's the danger, the adrenaline rush of cheating death… But Ryan soon realizes he's falling for her, hard. And he's powerless to stop it.

When the investigation and their attraction both heat up, Ryan must decide what's more important. Catching the killers? Or keeping Kelsey safe…

Grab your copy of *SEAL's Fake Relationship*
www.LeslieNorthBooks.com

~

EXCERPT

Chapter One

"Shooting down the walls of heartbreak…" Ryan Ward whispered before pulling the trigger.

Bang! Bang!

He glanced down the row at the paper target, two perfect holes straight through the center, and grinned, then tugged off his headphones.

"How the hell do you do that?" his brother Neal growled at him. All three brothers were sharing a single lane at the shooting range. It would have made more sense to line up separately so they wouldn't have to take turns—but then they couldn't mock and poke at each other while they were shooting which, obviously, was the most important part. "You're like the frigging Yoda of shooting or something," Neal said with a scowl. "You barely even looked at the target."

"When you've got it, you've got it," Ryan said with a smirk, stepping back to let Neal take his turn. "Not my fault I got all the sharpshooter genes while you got…hey, what *did* you get again?"

"'Gentlemen, you can't fight in here,'" their oldest brother, Lance, teased from behind them, quoting one of their favorite movies. "'This is the war room!' Or at least, a room with plenty of guns." Neal and Ryan just rolled their eyes. Ever since Lance had gotten back together with his ex-wife, who was pregnant with his child, he'd become a total goofball.

"So if we aren't going to fight, what are we supposed to do?" Neal asked, lining up his shot and then firing several times. "Hey, I know— we can talk about why Ryan's decided to leave his SEAL team."

"Nah, I think we should talk about how lousy your shooting has gotten. Think you might need glasses, bro?" Ryan examined the paper bullseye the machine had brought forward with mock concern. In truth, Neal was a good shot—all the Ward brothers were. But Ryan was the best. He never missed…except for metaphorically shooting himself in the foot.

It had been two and a half months since his final assignment with his SEAL team—since he'd charged in on a mission despite orders to stay put. It didn't matter that he hadn't been in the best headspace, having just learned his father had died. It didn't matter that his instincts had been *right,* and the mission would have failed without him. The navy had no use for a man who didn't follow orders. The best his CO could do was get him an honorable discharge, for mental health reasons.

Ryan snuck a look over at his two brothers, also former Navy SEALs. Neal had served with distinction until he'd been injured in the line of duty. Lance had put in twenty years with the navy and retired with full benefits. They were the best men he knew and he was proud to call them his brothers, but as the baby of the family, he'd spent his whole life trying to live up to their example. He wanted to wait a little longer before admitting to them just how badly he'd screwed up his military career. They could keep asking all they wanted—he would keep dodging their questions.

"Or maybe you just need some shooting lessons," Ryan suggested to Neal. "We could ask whoever's in that lane to our right—they're doing pretty well."

The person in there had been shooting since they got there, not saying a word, just firing and reloading and changing the bullseye, then starting again. Whoever they were, they had their headphones on and couldn't hear what the Ward brothers were saying anyway, so who cared. Ryan peered around the separator again at the anonymous shooter. At first, he thought it was a guy—on the short side, maybe half a foot shorter than Ryan's own six-foot-one. Slim, all dressed in black. Hair covered by a black ball cap and face obscured by the headphones and safety glasses and hat. Nothing that indicated gender one way or the other, but Ryan watched the person shoot, saw how they balanced against the recoil and realized it had to be a woman, based on the center of gravity.

His dad had been a private investigator and had taught Ryan plenty of tricks of the trade. Most especially trick number one: be observant. So he always had been. Sometimes, he'd use it as a party trick, showing off like Sherlock Holmes, but most of the time, he just quietly took note. The habit was so ingrained that he did it automatically. Without catching a glimpse of this person's face, he was already pretty sure he knew a number of things about her. She was practical, no frills.

Highly trained, definitely not a civilian, but not military. Law enforcement of some sort would be his guess.

There was also something oddly familiar about the person…

Bang! Bang!

He returned to his own stall and watched Lance take his turn before sneaking a peek at his watch. They'd been here for a few hours now and he was ready for a beer. "Our time's about up," he announced. "How about we get out of here? Want to grab a drink at Swingin' Sue's? I'll buy first round."

He put his gear away, half-listening to his brothers talk about their love lives. Neal was focused on his upcoming wedding to their dad's old assistant, Lori. Lance couldn't shut up about Ruth and the baby they were expecting. And Ryan…well, Ryan had his new self-appointed mission. It wouldn't exactly keep him warm at night, but it would give him a sense of purpose again. And that, way more than any romance, was exactly what he needed.

On that topic, he actually did want to update his brothers on what he had in mind. "Hey, I think I found something interesting going over the intel from Dad's case earlier. Pretty sure there's a dirty US Marshal involved. It would explain a lot."

His words rang out in the suddenly silent shooting range. The woman in the next lane must have been reloading.

Lance stopped stuffing things in his duffle bag. "Seriously?"

"Yep." Their father's case had been a tangled mess from the start, but they were in the last stage of it now. They'd found the person who had killed their father, while trying to make it look like a natural death. They'd found the person who'd ordered the hit in the first place—the mob boss who'd been angry at Dad's investigation into one of his criminal rackets. But there was one piece of the puzzle still missing. "We know that Russo wanted Dad out of the way once he started looking into those prison inmate deaths. But we still don't know who got to those prisoners in the first place. For my money, it must have been a US Marshal."

"Wow," Neal said, blinking at Ryan. Then he cursed and turned away, brows knit. "It's an interesting idea. But you know Lori and I can't really help you look into it, right? We've got a full caseload on top of our wedding planning. That doesn't leave us with much time to spare to chase down some theory for you, bro, just based on your hunch."

It was more than a hunch, but Ryan let it slide. He got how busy Lori and Neal were, now that they were running Dad's PI business together. And he knew they'd already done their part for the overall investigation. It was Lori who had first chased down the idea that Dad had been murdered, working with Neal to find out who had done it. Then Lance and Ruth had followed the trail of the man who had ordered the hit. Lance and Neal and Lori and Ruth had all put a lot of time and effort into those cases.

When Ryan didn't answer, Neal went on. "But I get the appeal of wanting to solve the final piece of the puzzle for Dad's last case. Especially since the trail's gone cold and the police have given up on it."

"Does anyone else think the Marshals are involved?" Lance asked, frowning.

Ryan took a deep breath and shook his head. "Nope. Just me, for now."

"Hmm." Lance picked at the front of his jacket. "And closing this case is really what you think you should be doing right now? Instead of going back to your SEAL team?"

Going back to his SEAL team wasn't an option, not that Lance knew that. All he'd told his brothers was that he'd decided to leave the military so he could focus on finishing this case. If they happened to assume that he'd *voluntarily* left the navy to work this investigation, that wasn't his fault. He hadn't actually said that—even if he'd maybe implied it, hoping to stop the questions about how he could still be on bereavement leave weeks after any real leave would have ended.

"Of course," Ryan said. This wasn't an avoidance tactic. He really did want to find out that last person responsible for their dad's death. Maybe then his grief would finally lessen over that whole thing, because damn. His chest still ached over it. Too much loss too close together. First Dad, then his SEAL team… He brushed it off, staring down at the graffiti-carved tabletop. "It's what's best for me."

Liar.

Lance paused a beat or two, then nodded, his expression unreadable as he finished securing his gun case and picked it up. "Because going down a rabbit hole trying to arrest every criminal in the city who's even tangentially related to Dad's death isn't what he would've wanted for you."

"I know that. I'm not an idiot, bro." His shoulders tensed, the muscles in his upper back knotting tight with frustration. Yes, he had other shit, important shit, going on, but that wasn't what was happening here. It wasn't. He wasn't avoiding what had happened. He was just letting it sit a bit, digest, then he'd deal with it all when the time came. There was the sound of shuffling feet from the stall on his other side, then a couple of clicks as the person reloaded. Still shooting away without a care in the world. *Lucky.* "Look, guys. I'm fine, okay? If neither of you wants to be involved in my investigation of the marshals, I'll do it myself. But for the record? It's not a wild goose chase. I've got a plan."

"Oh, Jesus." Neal shook his head, chuckling. "Not another plan."

"Right?" Lance said, laughing. "We've been down that road too many times with you, little bro."

Ryan flipped them both off, then sat forward, lowering his voice to avoid being heard in the quieter place. "Seriously. Just hear me out. I want to sneak into the local US Marshal's office to get a look at some files and—"

"And?" a voice said beside him, cutting him off. "Please go on describing how you plan to break into a law enforcement facility. That sounds like a really excellent idea to discuss, especially in public. No wonder your friends don't seem impressed by your planning skills."

He froze. That voice. He knew that voice. His heart sank as the woman from the next lane pulled off her hat to reveal long red hair and a face he knew all too well. His old high school nemesis, Kelsey Poppins.

Oh shit.

Grab your copy of *SEAL's Fake Relationship*
www.LeslieNorthBooks.com

Blurb

Never mix business with pleasure…

Keira Mantz just scored the job of a lifetime. She's been working for a high-end security company for years, and finally she has a mission all her own: to protect Erin, the Sheikh of Jawhara's wife. But what she thought would be a solo operation suddenly becomes a two-person job. And her partner is none other than Brock Wells, the man who recruited her. The last thing Keira wants is Brock stealing her thunder. But she'll do whatever it takes to succeed.

Brock has been avoiding Kiera since the night he found her fighting some very dangerous men in a bar parking lot. The Slade Security "no fraternization" rule is serious business, and with her mile-long legs, fierce determination, and unwavering focus, Keira is a temptation he can't afford. But with the threat to the sheikha closer than they realized, Brock and Kiera have to go deep undercover, posing as a couple. And suddenly that temptation becomes impossible to ignore…

When their ruse gets a little too real, can Keira and Brock risk letting their guards down? Or will giving in to their feelings put innocent lives in danger?

Grab your copy of *His Stubborn Lover*
www.LeslieNorthBooks.com

BLURB

Fate gave them a second chance at love…

Carolyn Evert couldn't take the sleepless nights that came with having a Navy SEAL fiancé, so she broke it off…then she discovered she was pregnant. After radio silence greeted her attempts to tell her ex-fiance Zach, Carolyn moved on with her life. But when she finds herself in a hostage situation at her jewelry store, she's shocked to see Zach arrive as part of a security response team.

The smoldering hot SEAL makes it clear he had no idea about the pregnancy, and Carolyn eventually agrees to let him into their son's life. But after all they've been through, she's still hesitant to let Zach back into her own heart.

Zach Vale won't let anything keep him from being the best dad he can be. He'll do whatever it takes to protect Carolyn and their son, and he soon discovers that the hostage situation wasn't an isolated incident. As they try to solve the mystery of who's behind the vicious attacks, Zach works to make himself part of their lives.

Can Carolyn and Zach listen to their hearts, and build a family together? Before it's too late...

**Grab your copy of *The SEAL's Surprise Son* (The Admiral's SEALs Book One) from
www.LeslieNorthBooks.com**

EXCERPT

Chapter One

"Just sold an engagement ring." Jenna poked her head in the office of All That Sparkles.

"Awesome." Carolyn Evert looked up from the spreadsheet she was studying. "Which one?"

"The one-carat heart-shaped diamond set in platinum." From the smile on Jenna's face, she was pleased with herself—and she should be. Both her commission and the store's profit would be very nice.

"I love that one." Carolyn sighed. "It's so romantic."

The ring had only been on display since the store reopened a week ago. Now that the remodel was complete, the neutral cream colors were gone. In their place Carolyn selected soft gray walls, chrome-edged glass display cases, modern recessed lighting, and pops of a vibrant blue for accent. The store did indeed sparkle.

"The couple looked at it yesterday," Jenna said with a knowing grin. "I knew they'd be back."

"You can always peg them. Congratulations."

"Do you want me to start the closing procedure?" Jenna asked.

Carolyn checked her watch. Ten minutes to close. "Sure. That'll be great. I want to get out of here on time tonight."

"Got it." Her most experienced salesperson scooted back out the door.

The thought of how the ring's sale would help the month's bottom line brought a smile to Carolyn's face as she returned to the spread-sheet. Her monthly expenses for All That Sparkles were significantly higher now due to a loan for the remodel and higher security costs.

She'd disagreed with her mother, Faith, about the expense. And maybe she was taking a chance, but she subscribed to the theory that you have to spend money to make it. The interior of a jewelry store reflected its reputation and merchandise, she felt. Faith had relented since she'd entrusted the store to Carolyn, who now held the reins.

Carolyn owed her mother so much. Faith had founded the store after Carolyn's father all but abandoned the family. Her hard work had put the business on the map in Sheridan Falls. Carolyn was in awe of someone who could do all that single-handed and raise two daughters, and she felt the pressure of measuring up to her mother's standard as she faced a similar life as a single mom and business owner. Her best efforts might not be enough even with the assistance of dedicated employees—but her self-doubt hadn't prevented her from taking a leap with All That Sparkles.

She heard the click of the alarm. Someone was being let into the office area of the store. A state-of-the-art security system had been an integral part of their refurbishment. It made her insurance company happy and gave her peace of mind, plus, it allowed them to carry top-end merchandise, such as the engagement ring Jenna was celebrating. It was worth it, she thought, even though she grimaced every time she pulled up the expenditures page.

"Mama," her son's voice called, bringing an instant smile to her face. A second later her babysitter entered the office with Austin on her hip, squirming to get down.

"Hi, baby." Carolyn took her fourteen-month-old son, hugging him tight to her and pressing her face into his thick dark hair that was so like his daddy's. With his deep blue eyes, no one could doubt who his father was, not that Zach Vale apparently cared. She suppressed a sigh. Silence had greeted her letters and communications to her ex-fiancé telling him that she was pregnant. After sending one last notification of Austin's healthy entrance into the world, Carolyn had stopped trying to contact Zach, who was off on a mission with his SEAL team. She couldn't change that, so she focused on her son. "Did you have fun today?"

Austin gave her a grin and showed her a toy tractor clutched in his hand, zooming it up her arm.

"He's been looking forward to coming all day," Nina said, dropping the bag of baby supplies on a chair. "He loves being here, and he loves his mama."

"Thanks for bringing him to me." Carolyn gave her son a kiss before setting him on the carpet to play. She'd felt guilty about working long hours while the store was being refurbished, because she'd promised herself she would never let him feel abandoned by a parent. Nothing she'd ever done to get her father's attention had been enough. She'd tried desperately to be the best student and best athlete, hoping he'd notice. She'd even begged her mother for martial arts classes because her father mentioned that he liked martial arts. She took classes for years, increasing her skills and moving on to grade after grade. Her father never once came to see her demonstrate her skills. Nothing had ever worked to get his attention.

She'd never let her son feel the way she had, which might be a struggle down the road. Eventually, she knew Austin would ask about his daddy. All children did. Whatever she decided to tell him, she'd be careful to never let it seem that he'd been unwanted.

"No problem," Nina said. "I love the new look of the store. The blue sets everything off. On our way here, we took a little stroll past Castle Jewels."

"Oh?" Carolyn's primary competitor had recently updated as well. "Is it nice?"

"Classy looking. Lots of gold accents. But it was kind of stuffy, too. I didn't feel like I could wander in and browse." Nina wrinkled her nose. "I think you made the better choice."

"Hope so." She watched Austin, who played with the tractor, running it over the pattern in the carpet and making goofy faces and sounds. He was so like his father, who despite being a SEAL loved the silly side of life, too. It had been her choice to end their relationship, but she couldn't help missing Zach. There was so much to love about him.

"I've got to get going," Nina said. "My boys have a baseball game tonight."

"I'll let you out through the secure door." Carolyn scooped Austin up and led the way to the showroom.

Just as they reached it, the front door flung open, slamming against the wall, and a man burst through, gun in hand. Carolyn froze in place, hoping this wasn't what it looked like.

"This is a robbery," he yelled, swinging his gun in an arc to encompass the store. "Hands where I can see them."

Carolyn took in a sharp breath, fighting the panic she felt. If the robber had entered five seconds earlier, she could have secured her son and Nina in the office, but they were all too visible. She pressed the tiny button on the key she always carried, triggering a silent alarm that contacted the police and her security firm. It also gave them a live audio and video feed.

"Everybody, down on the floor," the robber commanded. "Except you." He pointed to Jenna, who stood behind a display of their most expensive pieces.

Carolyn gestured for everyone to comply. It seemed safest to obey him while they waited for help to arrive. On her way down, she grabbed a pair of ear protectors left over from the remodel and slipped them on Austin's head. Maybe if her son couldn't hear the drama unfolding in front of them, he wouldn't be frightened. She smiled at him, whispering they were playing a game, hiding the fear that raced through her.

The robber, focused on shouting at Jenna to dump trays of diamonds and sapphires into a bag, didn't notice what Carolyn did or that she and Nina tried to cover Austin with their bodies. If the man walked closer, he'd see her little boy, but she'd do whatever was necessary to protect him.

She took a quick look around. Her other salespeople were on the floor, following procedure. They'd gone through training for this scenario, but these situations could go wrong very quickly. *Please let him get what he wants and get out*, she prayed. She winced at the sound of glass shattering as he smashed a display case of emeralds and shouted for Jenna to pick out the precious stones. Jenna worked quickly, filling the bag the robber held.

"Now, you get on the floor, too," he told Jenna, "and the rest of you stay down." He moved toward the door. It was going to be over more quickly than she'd expected. A few more seconds and he'd be out.

Carolyn tensed as the robber swung the heavy glass door open, revealing a swath of the street from where she lay. Police cars blocked the street. They'd arrived silently, which was protocol, but she could see the man panic at the sight. His means of escape was cut off.

He pivoted his head like an animal who had unexpectedly become prey to a larger beast before stepping back, slamming the door, and throwing the dead bolt. They were trapped in the store with an armed robber. The gun he carried swept across all of them, shooting fear through her heart.

Zach Vale attached the scope to his sniper rifle after taking up position on the second floor of a building directly across the street from All That Sparkles. The situation was going to challenge the calm persona he'd mastered as a sharpshooter on his SEAL team. He reminded himself that it was a job like any other. He didn't want to screw it up, and he sure as hell didn't want to tell his new boss the store he was watching through his scope belonged to his former fiancée. He'd get replaced by another sharpshooter ASAP—and no way was he letting someone else take his spot on this mission. Carolyn might have tossed him out of her life, but he'd do whatever he could to protect hers.

He evaluated his line of sight into the store. If the target showed himself in the front window, he'd be easy pickings. Zach used the scope, hoping to catch sight of the man. Nothing.

He didn't know if Carolyn was in there. It was likely, all his experience with her told him that. She prided herself on working hard. That was unlikely to have changed in the nearly two years since she'd ended their engagement.

He could barely think about that night. There had been no warning. She'd simply told him it was over because she could no longer take it that he chose his work as a SEAL over her. Never much of a talker, he'd been knocked speechless by her declaration. He'd thought what they had was special, the kind of love that could weather any storm. How wrong he'd been still stunned him. He should have known that type of love didn't truly exist.

To have Carolyn disrespect his job in the Navy—when he was convinced it had saved him from a life of crime—had sliced through him, and he'd been powerless to argue with her rejection. He'd thought she knew him well enough to understand his position as a sharpshooter was like breathing to him. How could she not have seen that giving him an ultimatum about his job was like asking him for his lungs?

"Vale, do you have a good position?" The sharp voice of his commanding officer came through his earpiece.

"Roger that. Front window is in range. I can take him if he shows."

"Stand by. Let the negotiator do his job, but don't let your guard down."

As if Zach would in any situation, let alone when the woman he'd once loved was likely feet from an armed robber. He pushed away the memory of Carolyn and their broken engagement. He had a job to do. He refocused, digging deep for the calm that was necessary to pull the trigger. Chatter on the radio told him negotiations weren't going well. The robber wouldn't speak to the police negotiator on the phone, the standard way of communicating in these situations.

Zach didn't want to think about how desperate a man would have to be to refuse a simple conversation, even if it was to tell the negotiator to go to hell. He wished he had the visual and auditory feed his commander did. Then he could be sure where Carolyn was. But all he had were his own eyes trained on a shiny glass window. He'd chosen his position because the glare was minimal, but it would still be a factor if it came to eliminating the target.

"In the window," Zach heard on the radio, but he'd already made visual contact through his scope. The robber's shoulder came into view: gray T-shirt, nothing remarkable, but he seemed to be dragging something. Zach increased the pressure on the trigger, waiting for more of the target to show. He almost had a clean shot when a blonde woman appeared in front of the man. His hands gripped her arms, pressing into her flesh and holding her in place in front of him.

She clutched a kid to her chest, her hand wrapped around his head. The boy was young, barely more than a baby, and wore red ear protection. Zach mentally cursed the robber for hiding behind a woman and child.

Although he already knew what he would see, Zach focused the scope on the woman's face to confirm her identity. Carolyn. Her brown eyes were wide in fear, and there was no sign of the dimples he'd always loved so much. He released his trigger finger as his breath caught in his chest. He'd never attempt the shot.

"Human shield," he said into his mic. "No clear target."

Grab your copy of *The SEAL's Surprise Son* (The Admiral's SEALs Book One) from www.LeslieNorthBooks.com